ICE AND FYRE

BRENDA BARRETT

ICE AND FYRE
A Jamaica Treasures Book/November 2024
Published by Jamaica Treasures
Manchester, Jamaica

This is a work of fiction. Names, characters, places, and incidents are either the product of the author's imagination or are used fictitiously. Any resemblance to an actual person or persons, living or dead, events, or locales is entirely coincidental.

All rights reserved
Copyright © 2024 by Brenda Barrett

No part of this book may be reproduced or transmitted in any form or by any means, electronic or mechanical, including photocopying, recording, or by any information storage and retrieval system, without permission in writing from the Publisher, except where permitted by law.

ISBN 978-976-8247-99-5

"Everything okay?" Pastor Shepherd asked, pulling out a chair for her to sit. "You had a faraway look in your eyes for a moment there. I hope all the food I bought was up to your standards."

"It is," Jody nodded. "I was baffled that you have all my favorites."

He smiled. "Well, then, we have something in common because all of them are my favorites. I am happy that you were around when I knocked on your door. Maybe we should explore what else we have in common, Miss Fyre."

Jody smiled. "I would like that."

"I also have dessert," he said. "Nothing fancy, just some cream-filled donuts and chocolate ganache ice cream because it is Sunday."

"Are you serious?" Jody asked excitedly. "You are not putting me on?"

"Is that something else that you like?" he asked cautiously.

"Yes!" Jody squealed. "Down to my favorite ice cream flavor of all time. Chocolate ice cream is boring, but chocolate ganache is something else."

"I am truly in awe," he said, "and more than a little intrigued that our tastes are so closely aligned."

ALSO BY BRENDA BARRETT

FULL CIRCLE
NEW BEGINNINGS
THE PREACHER AND THE PROSTITUTE
AFTER THE END
THE EMPTY HAMMOCK
THE PULL OF FREEDOM
REBOUND SERIES
THREE RIVERS SERIES
NEW SONG SERIES
BANCROFT SERIES
MAGNOLIA SISTERS SERIES
SCARLETT SERIES
WILEY BROTHERS SERIES
PRYCE SISTERS SERIES
THE JACKSONS SERIES
CRIMSON HILL SERIES
SPICE AND STONE SERIES
RIDGEVIEW SERIES

ABOUT THE AUTHOR

Brenda Barrett is an award-winning and bestselling author who has a passion for writing real Jamaican romances.

When she's not weaving words that transport readers to exotic locales, you can find her nurturing her green thumb in the garden or doting on her beloved cats.

With an infectious zest for life, this author brings a unique perspective to her writing that is both relatable and thought-provoking.

Don't be surprised if you find yourself lost in the pages of her latest work, as she seamlessly blends romance with some drama, mystery, and suspense, or even sci-fi, leaving readers wanting more.

You can connect with Brenda online at:
Brenalbar.com
Facebook.com/AuthorBrendaBarrett

Chapter One

Ice walked toward Saint's offices on the top floor of the Wiley Securities building. It was a Sunday, so it was deserted and felt like a ghost town. Usually, the place was a beehive of activity.

It was such a contrast to six months ago when he had returned after his undercover stint where he had helped capture criminal overlord, Milo, He had gotten a standing ovation from the first floor up to here.

They welcomed him home with enthusiasm and happiness. Even Saint Wiley, his boss and friend, had come out of his office and was standing like a proud father, smiling benevolently at him as he made his way down the plush carpeted hallway.

Ice smiled, thinking of the scene. It was a far cry from when Saint had recruited him to work for Wiley Securities. He had come to the job fresh out of law school with no intent to practice law and a skewed idea of what being a detective entailed. He had studied law because his parents wanted him to. His dad, Irving Carlisle Ellis, Senior, was a lawyer and loved it.

He had thought he would love it too. He liked the law, but he preferred the solving crime part of things.

Saint had laughed at his audacity that first day when he had declared that he had what it takes to be a detective because he had a law degree.

"Oh no, if you are going to work at this company, you must widen your skill set." Saint had declared. "All our men go through military training."

"Military training?" Ice had widened his eyes. "What on earth for?"

"A well-rounded detective needs more than just legal expertise. Military training helps develop discipline, physical endurance, and tactical skills. It prepares you for the unexpected, teaches you to think on your feet, and builds mental resilience. Plus, it adds an extra layer of protection when you're out in the field."

Six months of military training had not broken him. His instructors had told him at the get-go that they would break him down and build him back up. They tried; they really did. The harder they came for him, the more he was determined to succeed. By the end of the training, they were calling him Iceberg. What you saw was just the tip of it.

One of his trainers had asked him to join the military full-time after that stint, but Saint had other plans.

He spent five months of intensive training with some of the best detectives in the game, including Saint Wiley himself. It had been quite a wild ride. And he had enjoyed every moment of it.

He glanced at his appearance in the office glass. He barely looked like his regular self; bearded, long-haired, slimmer than he liked; he made a face. Even his mother didn't recognize him when she saw him this morning. He had succeeded at his last assignment, blending so well into the crowd someone would be hard-pressed to pick him out of a group.

Jody would recognize him like this. This was frequently how he had looked when moonlighting as a gangster in Black Lane, Jamaica's notorious ghetto.

Then he was known as King. He had saved her one night from being harassed by one of Milo's henchmen.

She had been grateful and had taken a reluctant interest in him. She was a quiet type of girl, an introvert through and through. Her parents were dead, so she grew up with her grandmother, who did not encourage her to mingle with the people in the community. Getting her to open up to him had been an uphill task. They kept the relationship platonic. He had no reason to still think about her, but thoughts about her crept into his head at odd times throughout the day. And he hadn't told his therapist about her.

He had been appointed a therapist to decompress after his undercover stint downtown. He discussed everything with him except Jody Fyre, his one emotional link to the hell hole. He dreamed of going back to Black Lane as himself and starting a relationship with her, but that would be a bad idea.

He had single-handedly caused the power dynamics in that area to topple and so he couldn't risk being exposed or putting her in danger if he showed up again, but he kept thinking about her and asking himself, was it love or just an attachment to the one person he had been almost honest with when he was undercover?

He wouldn't waste another minute thinking about Jody Fyre. Not another thought would be given to her cute face and kindly eyes.

Saint's office door was slightly ajar, so he knocked and stepped in.

Saint's office had a small conference room table at one end that could seat eight and a desk with four chairs at the other.

The conference table was in use. A harried-looking Saint stood at the top. Max Harry, the operations manager in charge of the undercover division and his immediate boss, was seated at the other end. In the middle was Bishop Cassius Monroe.

Someone had just killed the clergyman's children. It was a shocker to see him sitting at the table.

Saint looked up and called him over when he stepped into the room.

"Hey, Ice, sorry to drag you out of your warm bed this blessed Sunday."

Ice shrugged. Saint had no issues dragging him out of bed, day or night. It was just a polite way to greet him.

"I was at the gym," he said, "trying to bulk up. It is my latest obsession."

Max chuckled. He knew Ice's last undercover assignment had necessitated him losing weight. Ice had hated it and had been trying to gain weight ever since.

"This is Cassius Monroe," Saint introduced him to the pastor. "I was just telling him that you are one of our best undercover agents."

Ice nodded. "Ok."

"We can't use him," Cassius said belligerently, looking Ice up and down. "He looks like a thug."

"Ouch," Ice murmured, unperturbed by the comment.

"He cleans up well," Saint said, handing Ice a folder. "You may have heard that the bishop lost his two adult children last night. He called me at 3 am this morning, wanting us to handle the investigation."

"Oh," Ice said. He had a good poker face; he didn't let anyone around the table know that he had not only heard about the murders but he knew about the circumstances surrounding them.

Lydia Monroe and her brother Bishop Nathan Monroe were found in bed together, naked. They were killed that way, execution-style.

The file was thin and hastily put together. Wiley Securities was the security firm for the bishop's ministry. They had only rudimentary information on Lydia and Nathan, just the bare facts. When he was done, it wouldn't be this way.

He read the file quickly and then closed the folder. The information was just banal drivel. He had known Lydia personally; she had married his cousin, Charles. He was at their wedding. He also knew that she had painted the town red after their divorce.

One of his buddies had described her as insatiable, and he now knew that she was sleeping with her brother, and that had been the reason for the divorce.

"So, what do you require of me?" he asked out loud.

He looked at Saint, trying to avoid the bishop's sneer.

The bishop did not look like a man who was grieving. Maybe he was in the anger part of the grieving cycle, and everything and everyone ticked him off.

"We want you to go undercover as a counselor at the ministry," Saint said. "See what you can find."

Cassius snuffed. "The vacancy was for a pastor with a counseling degree. Do we have to use subterfuge to do this?"

Saint nodded. "Unfortunately, we do. You said you think the murderer was someone close to the family."

"Nathan's wife, perhaps," Ice said. "Isn't the wife always

the first suspect in crimes like these?"

"What do you mean, crimes like these?" Cassius sputtered. "What do you know?"

"They were having sexual relations at Lydia's apartment, and someone caught them," Ice said as respectfully as he could.

Cassius closed his eyes tightly and inhaled. "How do you know this?"

"A police buddy of mine called," Ice said. "They are keeping it hushed for now, but it will get out sooner or later. People talk. I heard about it barely an hour after it happened."

"Good grief," Cassius covered his face with his hands. "How will I live this down?"

"We can start by catching the guilty," Saint said. "In the meantime, we offer you the best detective we have on staff."

"Okay," Cassius murmured. "He has to be clean-shaven and can't wear those cane row things on his head. And is that a tattoo on his hand? It has to be covered up."

Ice looked at his guns and roses tattoo. "It's temporary. I had to do it for a job. As for the hair, I had to do it for a job too, and I can shave. When I am done, you won't recognize me from any other counselor minister you would hire."

"Oh," the bishop sighed in relief. "Sorry to criticize your appearance. It's just that we have a certain dress standard. People expect their religious leaders to dress and look a certain way."

"I understand," Ice nodded.

"When can he start?" the bishop asked Saint.

"Wait a minute," Ice said. "What exactly does a pastor/counselor do at your place? I will not be required to preach, will I?"

"No," Cassius looked at him like he had lost his mind.

"You will have an office and encourage the staff to speak to you."

"And in your role as a counselor," Saint said, "you will visit everyone on your suspect list. You are going to have to lay the groundwork on this one."

"Everyone is a suspect," Cassius said sadly. "Everyone."

****

The groundwork was laid shortly after Cassius Monroe left. Saint had called in the required staff. There were information analysts gathering data about Monroe Ministries and surveillance operatives combing through the surveillance systems, putting names to faces, and doing rudimentary background checks. The office was far from the silent place it had been earlier.

Saint had hauled the company tailor out of bed, and a barber was standing by to groom him. In a mere three hours, he was fitted with three suits and was cleanly shaven. His hair was trimmed low. He hadn't seen himself looking like this for a long time. He looked like one of the lawyers at his father's firm. Irving Carlisle Ellis, Sr., would shed a tear if he saw him like this now.

"I look like a lawyer," he said out loud to Saint and Max. They were lounging in chairs, watching as his transformation took place. They had casually chatted to each other, but now, as he strutted before them, they were silent, staring at him with various levels of incredulity.

"Not a lawyer," Saint frowned, "maybe a male model, fresh off the runway. You look like you should be on the cover of a magazine. Maybe we shouldn't have had the suits fit you so perfectly."

"It's not the suit," Max mused. "He looks chiseled,

handsome in a dangerous way like he is someone you don't want to mess with. Like he will sleep with your women and kill your men. A sophisticated spy."

Saint howled with laughter. "James Bond."

"James Bond," Ice adopted an English accent. "Will someone please send my audition tape to the showrunners?"

Max snickered.

Saint grinned. "You do that so effortlessly."

"And I will do the pastor thing effortlessly, too," Ice shrugged a well-tailored shoulder. "I will change my accent to a more pastorly one."

"We need to take this to the streets," Saint said. "Chanelle should be almost ready for us. I want you to be on the compound by evening."

Chanelle Lewis, the operations supervisor, and person in charge of his team, was on the phone when they walked in.

Her office door was open. She looked over at him and mouthed, "Wow."

"Give me thirty minutes," she covered the phone. "I am trying to work out the logistics of Ice staying at the complex where the murders happened."

Chapter Two

Saint, Ice and Max retreated to Saint's office to discuss what they knew about the murders. The key detective on the case briefed Saint as they sat waiting for Chanelle. They had the detective on speakerphone.

"Why are you guys interested in this?" Linton asked.

"Because," Saint said, "the bishop wants us to catch the bad guy and he doesn't trust that you guys will do it in good time."

"Fair enough," Linton said, unperturbed. "Our caseload is taller than the Wiley Securities Building. Are we going to get credit when you solve this?"

"Of course," Saint said. "We will bring you in when it's time to make an arrest. We'll turn over all the evidence to you, as usual."

"Such a pity you guys can't partner with us on more cases," Linton ruffled through his papers. "Oh, here it is."

"It was buried already?" Saint asked.

"Yes," Linton said, "unfortunately, this is not the only case we had in the corporate area in the early hours of Sunday morning. Let's see, female victim, aged twenty-nine years old, male victim, forty-five. They were both found naked in bed, with the female victim being the first target. We theorize that she was the first to be shot because she was closest to the door. Based on the shell casings found at the crime scene a 9mm handgun was used."

"Witnesses reported hearing multiple gunshots around 2:00 a.m. but did not observe anyone leaving the area. However, the sound was muted, as only the surrounding townhouses heard the shots, like heavy thuds and not an outright explosion."

"So, a silencer was used?" Saint asked.

"It would seem so," Linton said. "The crime scene was processed for physical evidence, and several items were collected for further analysis. These included the shell casings, which will be sent to the ballistics lab to determine if they match any other firearms involved in previous crimes."

Saint groaned, "Can you send it to us? You guys take months to do forensic analysis."

"Sure thing," Linton said, "as soon as I get the requisite permission. Since you are on this, we will try to swiftly process the DNA samples that were taken from the victims."

"Thank you," Saint breathed.

Linton chuckled. "Our detectives will gather statements and look at potential leads later today. But so far, we have no eyewitnesses. The neighbor to the right is away for the weekend; she is Miss Maci Graham. The neighbor to the left is a Bishop Heneghan and his family, who are on a month's vacation to Thailand. Apparently, that is where his wife is from."

"What about cameras?" Saint asked.

"The cameras around the townhouse are not working," Linton said.

"Quite a coincidence," Saint murmured.

"I expect you will probably sort out why long before I do," Linton said. "I am happy you are working with the police on this one. Keep me posted."

"Of course," Saint hung up.

"There you have it, folks." Ice sighed. "I'll have my work cut out for me."

"Knock, knock," Chanelle came to the door. "I heard you talking to Linton and waited until you were done."

"Come on in," Saint said.

"I can't believe how handsome you look!" Chanelle said to Ice. "My goodness, were your cheekbones always so chiseled?"

Ice ran his hand across his cheekbones and chuckled. "Apparently, this guy has been hiding under my scruff for a while."

"I like him," Chanelle grinned. "You have the perfect face for detective work. One minute you look convincingly like an evil villain and the next, you are a holy man. We should find something for you to do in the fashion industry next."

Saint chuckled. "What do you have there, Chan?"

Chanelle placed the thick file on the desk. "We did some grunt work in laying the foundation for Pastor Shepherd so that he doesn't go into this blind."

"Shepherd?" Ice frowned. "Isn't that name too on the nose?"

"It is, and that's why we chose it. It's easy to remember, and no one there has that name." Chanelle said. "Your profile sheet is right here."

She handed him the sheet.

"Your undercover name is Pastor John Shepherd. You are

28 years old, you graduated from the seminary magna cum laude, you have a master's in counseling and psychology, and you wear glasses."

"Glasses?" Ice grinned. "Now, this is a first."

"It will make you look more approachable," Chanelle said. "That's what our new detective AI says you should wear to be more convincing as an undercover pastor."

She handed him a case with a pair of glasses in it. "It worked for Superman. He fooled everybody into thinking that he was Clark Kent with just glasses. It's plain glass, don't worry."

"Here is a mirror," Saint handed him a mirror that was on his desk. "Try it on."

"I'll never understand why nobody worked out that Superman and Clark Kent were one and the same. It's not like he looked much different," Ice murmured.

"People see what they expect to see," Chanelle replied. "They perceive reality based on their preconceived notions and beliefs."

Ice put on the glasses and looked at his reflection. "You have a point. I do have a certain trustworthy air to me now."

"You do," Saint laughed. "Good old glasses coming through."

"It was the missing piece to the outfit," Max agreed.

"So, for this assignment, your goal is to blend in and gain the trust of those you interact with. The combination of your trustworthy-sounding name, Pastor John Shepherd, and the glasses will help create an approachable and non-threatening persona," Chanelle said. "We arranged for you to stay in apartment 1B, beside Tawny Monroe's secretary. The previous tenant is on vacation and had plans to move out. We expedited that.

We wanted you to stay in the townhouse section, but they

are all occupied. We could only get you near the admin staff."

"I see," Ice nodded. "So there are townhouses and apartments over there?"

"Yes," Chanelle said. "Monroe Ministries owns the apartments and townhouse complex that's next to the church compound. There are twenty townhouses on one side. That's where their senior staff and family stay, rent-free. It's a perk of the job."

"And on the apartment side, there are thirty, one and two-bedroom apartments where they house staff as well. It is a gated complex with no manned security at the gate. All the residents have a key fob to open the gate, so it is not a scenario where you can just walk in. They have cameras around the property. They are on a seven day overwrite cycle."

"The bishop just had his operations manager send over the tapes. We combed through the past seven days, and curiously, the cameras pointing to the townhouses have been malfunctioning for weeks. The person in charge of operations ordered replacements, and they just arrived yesterday."

"That's what Linton just confirmed," Saint said.

"How ironic," Ice murmured. "Lydia and Nathan were killed right before the new cameras went up. It sounds like someone was biding their time and decided it was now or never."

"That's exactly what I thought," Chanelle nodded. "We do have something, though. At around eleven o'clock, Bishop Nathan Monroe was seen coming out of apartment 1C on the ground floor of the apartment building. Those cameras are still working. Apparently, he was visiting Tawny Monroe's assistant. He got there at ten and left ten minutes later."

"Interesting," Ice murmured. "So he was cheating on his wife with his sister and his mother's assistant? What's in the water at Monroe Ministries?"

"So the secretary is the main suspect as of now?" Ice raised an eyebrow.

"According to the surveillance tapes," Chanelle said. "As of now, she is the last recorded person to see Nathan Monroe."

"Okay," Ice nodded. "She is going to the top of my suspect's list. What's her name?"

"Jody Fyre," Chanelle said.

Everything in Ice stilled. "Say that name again?"

"Fyre," Chanelle looked down at her files. "You know her?"

Ice nodded. "As a matter of fact, I do."

"Oh no," Saint groaned. "How well does she know you? Does she know the debonair, modelesque Ice in front of us or undercover persona Ice?"

"Persona Ice. I am sure she won't recognize me though," Ice said. "I was King when she met me in Black Lane. One evening I rescued her from two of Milo's goons while she was coming home from work a little later than usual, so I started looking out for her when she got in late."

"Are you sure she won't recognize you?" Saint asked.

"Sure," Ice nodded. "Very sure. My face was bearded, my hair was in locks, I was skinnier, and I was using a different accent. Besides, I wore shades most of the time; I was fully living my King character. When I befriended her, we mainly saw each other at night or late evenings. I picked her up a couple of times from her job if she was working late, and we would have a meal in my car. She was deathly afraid of her grandmother seeing her talk to a gangster."

"Did you sleep with her?" Max asked.

"No," Ice said. "It was purely platonic. We never even kissed. I was on my best behavior. Jody doesn't seem like the type to have affairs, though. She was so sheltered, she acted like she was from her grandmother's era."

"She certainly doesn't fit the profile of a murderer," Chanelle said, skipping through her pile of files and finding the page dedicated to Jody. "She has a pretty boring life, actually. Until four months ago, she had a Black Lane address. She is twenty-four years old. She has an associate degree in business administration and worked at Thelman and Associates as an administrative assistant for three and a half years."

"That's about right; that's a law office downtown. Her boss was Yanique Thelman, a woman who she greatly admired. She was both a mother figure and a boss rolled into one."

"Miss Thelman migrated to Canada," Chanelle said, "and she arranged for Miss Fyre to work with an old friend, Tawny Monroe."

"Ah," Ice nodded, "makes sense. What doesn't make sense is how the Jody that I knew and was looking out for, for more than two years would end up in an affair with a married man and be passionate about him to kill him in a mere three months."

"It doesn't add up," Chanelle said doubtfully. "But people can change. I will be doing a thorough background check on her for sure."

"You sound like you formed an attachment to her," Saint said. "Please don't blow your cover."

"I won't," Ice said. "I am a professional."

"In the meantime," Chanelle said, "I will be testing out the new detective software that Gary from IT has been gunning for me to try. It can analyze vast amounts of data and cross-reference it with our suspect list. It should help us identify any patterns or connections we may have missed. It should cut our work in half in figuring out who did this."

"That sounds promising," Max chimed in. "The more information we have, the better chance we have of cracking this case."

Chanelle nodded. "Exactly. This new software can help us focus on the most relevant leads and streamline our investigation. We need to stay one step ahead."

"I can do that," Ice said. "I am giving this case two weeks tops. If it's someone in the family, I'd say one week."

"And here is some bedtime reading," Saint took out a book from his desk drawer with the name Monroe Family Values by Tawny Monroe on the front. It had a picture of Cassius and Tawny Monroe and their children when they were younger. Nathan was standing to his father's right, and Lydia was a wee little thing with two ponytails.

Ice rolled his eyes, "Is this fiction or nonfiction?"

"You interact with them and tell us," Saint said.

Chapter Three

"**H**ello," Jody reached for her cell phone groggily. It felt as if she had just fallen asleep. What time was it?

"Jody, it is Tawny Monroe."

"Mrs. Monroe," Jody swiped her hand over her eyes and looked at the bedside table clock. It was six thirty.

"Listen carefully," Tawny said briskly. "I want you to forget what you heard in the office on Thursday night between me and Nathan. Do not mention it when the police ask you anything. They were not nice words, and it is not who we are as a family."

"The police?" Jody whispered. "Why would the police ask me anything?"

"Nathan and Lydia are dead," Tawny said, her voice caught on a sob. "I am surprised you aren't gawking outside like the rest of the neighbors, looking at my children's lifeless bodies like a spectacle."

"I didn't know this," Jody was fully awake now. She pulled

herself out of bed and looked through her window. Quite a few people were milling around, and an even greater crowd was gathered in the townhouse section of the complex. There were flashing police lights, and a crime scene 'do not cross' tape was visible in the distance.

"My goodness," she said out loud. "How did it happen?"

"They were gunned down in the early hours of the morning. There was no sign of forced entry," Tawny sniffed.

"I am so sorry to hear, Mrs. Monroe," Jody said. "I can't imagine how you must be feeling now."

"Thank you," Tawny said, tears still evident in her voice. "This changes nothing between us. You are still fired. I can't have you around. You know too much about my family."

"Okay," Jody said slowly.

"I will give you a glowing recommendation to whoever you work for after this if you keep your mouth shut about what you heard on Thursday. You know how to keep secrets, Jody. After all, you were involved with a gangster."

Was that a subtle threat?

"Fine," Jody sat on her bed. "Can I be released from the obligatory month I have to work with you after this?"

"No," Tawny was horrified. "I need you around. We are almost finished with the book, and I need somebody in the office I can trust, fielding my calls, and doing what needs to be done, especially now that we have this tragedy. I will reward you generously for being loyal, Jody."

Hush money, Jody thought in dread.

"Okay, Mrs. Monroe," she said out loud. "I will not tell the police what I heard on Thursday."

"Good." Tawny hung up, and Jody sat staring at the wall. Her eyes felt gritty.

She hadn't slept much since Thursday night, ever since she had witnessed the blow-up between Mrs. Monroe and her son, Nathan.

Friday was the day when she was fired. She had been asked to leave in the nicest possible way because she had been privy to information she was not supposed to know. Mrs. Monroe could not handle anyone around her knowing the true state of her family life, especially her secretary, who was responsible for transcribing her books.

Jody had stayed up all Friday night planning and plotting her next moves. She dreaded returning to the inner city, even for a short time. She needed to find a job quickly so that she could seamlessly continue her life outside of that area.

And then, last night, Nathan showed up at her door to explain and apologize. She had told him she needed no apologies. She reassured him that she wouldn't say a word to anyone.

And today, he was dead. He and Lydia.

This felt surreal.

She had honestly thought that moving uptown to a church compound, no less, would be paradise. She had considered it an answer to prayers, her 'get out of the ghetto' card. People were the same wherever they lived, whether in the ghetto, uptown or between. It was naïve on her part to think a church compound would be a utopia.

Who would want them dead, though?

She was curious but wouldn't go outside and gossip with people.

She felt a shudder at the pit of her stomach, a delayed reaction to the news. She didn't even know why she was reacting this way. She was used to death and mayhem. Both her parents were killed when she was younger.

Jody closed her eyes. So many acquaintances and loved ones were lost to gun crimes. Her parents, her uncle, and now Lydia and Nathan Monroe.

She had genuinely thought that working in a Christian environment would have been heavenly. At least it was far from the noisy, crime-riddled bowels of the inner city where she was from.

The saying all that glitters is not gold had taken on real significance for her. On the surface of it, Monroe Ministries was gold, and to some people, it probably still was. She had just had the misfortune of working with Tawny Monroe, which meant she was closer than most to where the true action was.

She remembered her first day vividly. It was just six months ago. She had dressed in her best suit, a pinstripe black skirt, and a fitted jacket that her grandmother had sewn, which could rival any brand name suit.

She had entered the impressive seven-story Monroe Ministries building in New Kingston. It was modern in design and seemed to sparkle in the sun. She had paid a taxi man to take her straight to her location, and even he was impressed with the place.

"My daughter has always wanted to work here," he said. "I hear they pay well. Far above other people. Even their janitors make bank."

"I hope so," Jody said nervously.

She had heard the rumors too. Everybody had. What made the Monroes different from other heads of mega-churches was that they spread their money around. They didn't buy jets and expensive cars and flash their money around like they were religious rock stars. They invested in their people, created scholarships, and supported various charitable causes.

No wonder their organization had gained a reputation for offering attractive compensation packages.

Jody couldn't believe it when her previous boss, Yanique

Thelman, told her she was leaving for Canada but had already found her a position as a personal secretary to Tawny Monroe, the first lady of the Place of Love Worship Center and vice president of Monroe Ministries.

It was a more comprehensive role than the one she had with Yanique. Her duties would be diverse, and her hours would be punishing because Tawny Monroe was a woman with several fingers in many different pies. Monroe Ministries was a considerable concern, and besides that, Tawny had her own personal things on the side. She wrote several self-help books, mainly about families, and had a popular podcast called "Family Togetherness."

Jody navigated her way through the bustling lobby. A sign on the ground floor said, "To the Place of Love Worship Center: Main Chapel." Other signs pointed to the children's chapel, gift shop, and cafeteria.

It felt like a mall but with a church and university in it. She resisted the urge to check out the auditorium-sized church. She had always seen it on television but never in real life. There would be time for that if she got the job.

She made her way to the elevators instead. She didn't want to be late. She went to the middle one and pressed the button for the seventh floor.

"Good morning," a gentleman in a suit, cleanly shaved and smelling good, stood beside her.

"Good morning," Jody smiled.

"Going up to the seventh floor?" he asked, smiling.

He had nice teeth and a beautiful smile. He was handsome in a clean-cut kind of way. He had a sprinkling of grey at his temples. He was probably in his late thirties or early forties.

"I am," Jody nodded. "I have an interview with Mrs. Monroe."

"First Lady Monroe?" he raised his eyebrows.

"Yes," Jody smiled.

"You are pretty," he leaned his head to one side, "and young."

"Well, er, thank you, I guess," Jody frowned. "Is that a bad thing?"

"No," he said, "but the last pretty lady she had as a secretary got into trouble with her son, Nathan."

"Bishop Nathan?" Jody gasped. "But he is married!"

"That does not stop Nathan," the man shrugged. "If you don't want to get in trouble like the other secretaries before you, I suggest that you never smile with him. Be polite, be pleasant, but don't laugh at his jokes. Treat him like the womanizing scum that he is. Do not let down your guard. If you have to, quote the Bible at him, let him think you are a fanatic. He doesn't like fanatics, but you are pretty; he may make an exception for you."

Jody gasped. "Well, er, thank you."

"Don't mention it," the man said. "I wish I had warned the lady before you. She committed suicide when he broke it off with her."

Jody gasped. "Are you serious?"

"As a judge," the man nodded.

They went into the empty elevator together, and Jody turned to him. "What's your name?"

"Zahir Stevens, Youth Ministries Director," he grimaced. "Unfortunately, my sister was the secretary before you. She killed herself because of that man."

She opened her mouth. "Oh."

"Nathan is one of the worst human beings to walk this planet. He cannot be trusted. He will find you if you work on this floor, so don't trust him. Consider yourself warned."

Jody swallowed.

The elevator doors opened when it got to the seventh

floor, revealing a polished reception area with a receptionist behind a sleek desk. Zahir Stevens headed into the inner sanctum with a swipe of his card.

Jody approached the reception desk, feeling out of sorts.

She introduced herself and explained her purpose for being there. The receptionist nodded and told her to have a seat. Mrs. Monroe was on a call.

Jody sat down and picked up one of the Monroe Ministry magazines. It was their fortieth year of celebration. She started to read and enjoy seeing the before and after pictures. They had come a long way from their earlier days.

The business of religion was obviously profitable. She read through the profiles of several board members and started people-watching, trying to match the faces to the names in the magazine. Only the top members of the executive and their secretaries had offices on the top floor. She saw the bishop, Cassius Monroe himself, pass by. He looked taller than he did on television and younger, much younger than she had thought he would be.

But then the receptionist greeted him as Benjamin, and then she realized that it was his son. They really looked alike.

He felt her stare, turned around, stared back at her, and smiled.

She didn't know if she should smile back. That warning about Bishop Nathan from Zahir Stevens had her uncertain. Should she be smiling with any of the Monroe men?

Luckily, he was distracted by the receptionist. She breathed a sigh of relief.

She saw some sleekly dressed people come and go. A beautiful woman in a business suit, who oozed sophistication, stopped at the reception desk.

"Did Pastor McGowan leave anything for me, Annette?"

she asked. "I told him to drop it off up here. Don't want the nosy people on the second floor to know my business."

So the receptionist's name was Annette. Jody watched out of the corner of her eye as Annette checked under her desk.

"Yes, he did. Here it is, Miss Lydia," Annette said, handing the woman a package.

"Thank you," Lydia squealed. Then she looked over at Jody and frowned. "Who is she?"

"That's Miss Jody Fyre. She has an interview with your mother in five minutes."

"Ah, the replacement for poor Ziya."

Lydia approached her and smiled, but the smile didn't reach her eyes. She was checking her out like she was a competitor in a sport.

Jody tried to put her face in pleasant lines.

"All the best," Lydia said. "You are going to need it in these here streets."

Jody nodded. "Thank you."

Lydia laughed and headed to the elevator.

Jody should have followed her, walked out of the building, and never looked back. Instead, she waited, getting increasingly nervous, until a plump woman, probably in her mid-thirties, with low-cut curly hair in a grey suit, came over to her and smiled.

"Jody Fyre? My name is Marissa Callum. I will show you to Mrs. Monroe's office."

Chapter Four

The inner sanctum of the seventh floor was unlike anything she had ever seen: carpeted hallways lined with artwork and adorned with tasteful sculptures. Soft, warm lighting casts a comforting glow, creating an atmosphere of sophistication and prestige. It was a seamless blend of luxury and professionalism. Jody couldn't help it; she was excited. She wanted to work here in these offices. She couldn't imagine losing the awe she felt right now. Everybody who worked there must feel privileged.

She passed a glass-walled conference room and saw a group engaged in an animated discussion. She could just imagine the important conversations that took place within those walls, decisions that impacted lives and communities.

Marissa glanced across at her as if reading her mind. "It's a nice place to work; super busy, though. Mrs. Monroe's office is at the opposite end of Bishop Monroe's office, and there are various directors and VPs between. Here we are."

Jody looked around. Tawny Monroe's outer office had a large cubicle for her secretary and a window with a distant view of the Blue Mountains. It was a comfortable workspace.

"That's my temporary desk," Marissa said, smiling. "Who knows, after the interview, it might be yours permanently. If you get the job, we should celebrate at lunch."

Jody nodded. She liked Marissa instantly.

When she entered the office, she saw Mrs. Monroe tapping away at her laptop. She looked up when Jody approached. She looked the same as on television: straight as an arrow nose, high cheekbones, almond-shaped eyes, and nut-brown skin. Jody's grandmother called her the religious Angela Bassett. They did resemble a bit. It was impossible to say what age she was; the lady was quite simply ageless looking.

"Yanique did not say you were so pretty!" There was disappointment on her face after giving Jody a thorough once-over.

Jody swallowed. She didn't know if she should preen at the compliment or apologize that she was pretty. What was wrong with being attractive in this building? Were all attractive secretaries stereotyped as homewreckers that automatically fall at the feet of Nathan Bishop?

"Don't mind me," Tawny sighed. "I am sorry about that. Have a seat."

Jody sat down.

"I already know that you are a dedicated worker. Yanique has sung your praises enough. She said you were loyal to a fault, you don't indulge in gossip, and that she would have taken you to Canada if she could."

Jody nodded. "All of that was true," she said out loud. "I really enjoyed working with Miss Thelman. I am happy to hear she felt the same."

"Well then," Tawny sighed, "I have three questions for

you. Are you currently in any relationship?"

"No," Jody said.

Tawny raised an eyebrow. "Why not? You are an attractive girl."

"Well, I..." Jody inhaled. Should she tell her that she had spent the last two years of her life fantasizing about a gangster in her area, who may or may not be dead? And that she still spent way too much time thinking about him when she should be trying to forget him?

"I haven't found the right person yet," she finished weakly.

"What are your views on dating married men?" Tawny asked, squinting at her.

"Married men?" Jody shook her head. "Surely, married men and dating shouldn't be in the same sentence. Unless he is going on a date with the woman he married."

Tawny smiled. "Good answer. I am depending on you to remember that while working here. It pains me to say this, but some people here are not converted Christians. We built this ministry knowing that we are dealing with human beings. We have a tendency to err. Do you understand what I am saying?"

"I think so," Jody nodded.

"If I find that you are involved in a romantic relationship with anyone on this floor, I am firing you, no questions asked."

Jody nodded. "Okay."

"The position comes with housing," Tawny continued. "Our new housing complex is just next door. The commute is short. We offer all our staff free breakfast and lunch. Everybody is welcome to use the recreational facilities. We have tennis courts, basketball, football, squash—you name it, it's available."

Jody did a little squeal of happiness in her head.

"I hope you enjoy your time here and that we will get along quite well. You are to be loyal to me first and the Monroe family next," Tawny leaned forward. "And now my third question: Do you know the definition of loyalty, Jody?"

"Yes," Jody nodded. "Support, allegiance, always have your back."

"I like that," Tawny smiled, her perfect white teeth looking blindingly unreal. "You will have my back, whatever the situation."

****

She had gotten the job, and at first, she hadn't seen what all the hoopla was about. She met Nathan Monroe; he had seemed friendly enough. He didn't seem creepy or weird at all. He was handsome in an understated kind of way. He looked more like his mother than his father. His smile completely transformed his face, and he was super friendly.

"I heard Mom has new staff," he smiled at her. "How are you? My name is Nathan Monroe. Your neighbor, just a few doors down."

Jody smiled politely. "I am Jody Fyre."

"I like your hair," he moved closer. "What's that style again?"

"Mini twists," Jody said, touching her long hair. She was particularly proud of it. She had started her twist hairstyle years ago in high school, and her hair had grown to her mid-back. It was so long and thick; people usually thought it wasn't her real hair.

"It's pretty," Nathan smiled. "I should tell my wife about you. She has been inquiring about a natural hair hairdresser. Maybe you can tell her who yours is."

"I do it myself," Jody said. "It usually takes me a whole

day to do the twists, and I keep the style for three months."

"Mmm," Nathan smiled. "Talented and pretty."

When he left the outer office and entered his mother's office, Marissa shook her head. "Stay away from that man; avoid him as much as possible."

"Why is everybody warning me off him?" Jody asked. "He seems okay. He was just being friendly."

"I'll tell you more after work," Marissa said through gritted teeth.

Marissa had stuck around for two days to show her the ropes. Usually, she worked for Bishop Zahir Stevens. He was the one who had warned her about Nathan at first. She knew Marissa's views would reflect his; she spoke about Bishop Stevens in glowing terms every chance she got.

Marissa was happy that Jody had gotten the job; at their first lunch together, she shared her thoughts on Tawny Monroe's workload.

"It's unreasonable," Marissa said, "I will say a prayer for you; I can't wait to go back to Bishop Stevens' office. I can leave at five, arrive a little late, and no early morning phone calls or late-night practices for some grand speech she needs to give about her family. If you ask me, Lady Tawny needs two assistants.

"She has too much going on. I can't keep up. Good luck to you and this job. You must keep her schedule straight, write her speeches, transcribe her books, and fact-check and research them."

"That requires specialized editing skills. I told her I couldn't do that while fielding her calls. She gets a million calls daily, and she expects me to organize her travel arrangements, manage her email inbox, and coordinate meetings with important clients and stakeholders.

"And she is always guest speaking somewhere or the other,

and you have to listen to her speeches and give her feedback. She needs a team, I tell you. It's simply overwhelming for one person."

Jody smiled. "It sounds like fun."

Marissa shook her head. "Her last secretary took her life. I think it is partly due to the job."

Jody's smile wavered. "It's that bad?"

Marissa cackled wickedly. "You'll see. Did Lady Tawny give you the loyalty speech and having her back?"

Jody nodded.

"That's just to ensure that you don't complain while she kills you with work," Marissa said. "I will tell you more when we are not in this place. You never know who is listening."

****

"**I**t's nice in here!" Marissa had opted to visit her in her new one-bedroom apartment. It had an open-plan kitchen, living room, and tiny dining area. The place was furnished with basic pieces.

Jody wasn't finished unpacking. It was just two days since her move-in.

"They don't have any cameras in here, do they?" Marissa asked, looking around.

"I haven't seen any," Jody frowned. "Would they do that, though?"

Marissa laughed uncomfortably. "I don't know. I have been working with Monroe Ministries for ten years now, and I would not put anything past them."

"What do you mean?" Jody sat across from Marissa.

"I hear rumors. Of course, some of them may not be true, but I am sure many are. Do you have anything to drink?

This is going to take a while."

"I have June plum juice," Jody got up. "My grandmother made it from scratch."

"Ooh, yes," Marissa nodded.

Jody shared the drink and then said hesitantly, "I promised Mrs. Monroe that I wouldn't gossip, but I have been dying to know what happened to the secretary before me and why everybody is warning me off Nathan, a married man of the cloth."

Marissa took a sip of the drink and nodded. "Nathan loves pretty younger girls. He never tried anything with me. I am probably too old and too chunky for him. His wife, Terry, starves herself to maintain the skinny look he loves. That woman is always hungry, but she won't eat. She has this fetish where she likes to watch you eat. She'll go down to the cafeteria, order a small cup of soup, and sit and watch people eat while licking her lips longingly."

"That's awful," Jody said.

Marissa chuckled. "They have two sons, Nolan and Nesbeth. One's thirteen, the other fifteen. They prefer hanging out with their grandfather than with their own parents or grandmother. After working with Tawny for a while, you will realize that she is not overly motherly, though she talks about family all the time.

"Bishop Cassius is obviously more into the family than she is. He goes to lunch with his children, to the grandkid's various functions, and does everything you would expect his wife to do. I guess she's too busy telling people how great their family is to actually do family things."

"But she writes a lot of family-oriented books," Jody sputtered, "about clean living and having a close family unit."

"It's all fiction to her, I guess," Marissa said. "This juice is good."

"I'll be sure to tell my grandma," Jody said.

"Okay, here is all I know," Marissa took another sip of her drink. "Bishop Cassius is having an affair or had an affair with Mariam Graham, his secretary. Mariam's daughter Maci is supposedly his daughter. I don't know how true that is, but Maci was promoted the other day to HR director, and she does resemble Bishop Cassius quite a bit."

"Are you serious?" Jody whispered. "Not Bishop Cassius."

"Oh yes," Marissa nodded. "That's not all. Bishop Cassius' only acknowledged daughter, Lydia, quietly divorced a year and a half ago. And they tried to shut it down, but people whisper about these things. It is almost certain that she was cheating on her husband."

"I saw her in the reception area," Jody said. "She is pretty."

Marissa snorted. "She is a slut."

"No," Jody shook her head, "don't say that."

"It's true," Marissa said. "She is the female equivalent of Nathan. They are like two peas in a pod. I heard her behavior has gotten so bad, the bishop threatened to cut her off financially and ordered her to live here in the new complex where he can keep an eye on her, surrounded by his staff and other bishops."

Jody gasped. "No."

"Yes," Marissa cackled. "I saw her car over in the townhouse section, so there must be some truth to it. He owned the townhouse she was living in before. So she has to do what her daddy says because she can't afford to be cut off."

"But she's twenty-nine, an adult," Jody said.

"And she depends on her daddy dearest for everything, and he indulges his little princess," Marissa smirked. "I have no love for Lydia. I would act better if I had a daddy to indulge me like she does. She pretends to work in the admin office but keeps some erratic hours. It's her parents' business; I guess she can do what she wants. Do you have any crackers?"

Jody got up. "I do; that's about the only thing I have. I need to go shopping."

"It's fine. Once you have crackers, you have something," Marissa took the crackers and started chewing. "As for Nathan, he is a mess. The secretary before you, the one who killed herself, her name was Ziya Stevens, Bishop Stevens' sister."

"Are you sure he was the reason she killed herself?" Jody asked skeptically. "I mean, there could be several reasons."

"Yup, I am sure. She left a note in her apartment professing her undying love for Nathan and how she can't go on anymore," Marissa shook her head. "Anyway, her brother, Bishop Stevens, was briefly engaged to Lydia Monroe. It wasn't official or anything, but she was floating around the office with a big rock on her finger. She would come to his office like every other hour when they were seeing each other. The two of them were nauseating. It drove Bishop Nathan crazy. He used to scowl at them and make snide remarks. I have concluded that he doesn't like seeing his sister happy."

Jody frowned. "But why?"

"No clue," Marissa shrugged. "I got a feeling that was why he started pursuing poor, overworked Ziya Stevens. She was a delicate soul, the sweetest girl. Why couldn't he have left her alone?"

"But why did she succumb to him?" Jody asked. "She could have reported him for harassment."

"She wouldn't have done that," Marissa shrugged. "The poor thing thought she was in love. And then Lydia dropped

Bishop Stevens for reasons unknown, and then Nathan dropped Ziya, and just like that, she killed herself three weeks ago."

"Oh wow," Jody muttered.

"I don't know what is going on with Nathan and Lydia Bishop," Marissa scoffed, "but both are toxic. Stay away from them."

Chapter Five

Jody zoned back into the present when she heard a knock on her door.

"Miss Fyre, it's the police. We just want to ask you some questions."

When you have lived in a war zone for most of your life, 'it's the police' is not something you want to hear.

She took a deep breath, gave herself a look over in the mirror, and headed to the door. Tawny Monroe's voice echoed in her head from their phone call. "Keep your mouth shut about what you heard on Thursday. You know how to keep secrets, Jody. After all, you were involved with a gangster."

She should never have told Tawny Monroe about King because she now felt like she had something to hide.

They had been pulling a late-nighter in the conference room, where Tawny was practicing her speech for a huge women's conference at the Place of Love Center. She was the keynote speaker.

Jody had to stick around to put together the final draft. Tawny kept adding and subtracting little pieces of the document. During one of their breaks, Tawny turned on the television to watch the news.

Milo's trial was mentioned, and things were not looking good for the gangster. Even the US wanted him for crimes in their country.

"Isn't Black Lane where you are from?" Tawny had asked her absently.

"Yes," Jody said distractedly.

As usual, whenever Milo was mentioned, she listened keenly for anything related to King, hoping to hear if others were caught or dead.

She didn't even realize she was holding her breath until Tawny cleared her throat. Jody looked at her blankly. Her heart rate, as usual, was elevated.

"You know these people?" Tawny asked.

"No, not really," Jody said. "I kept my distance."

"Mmmm," Tawny murmured. "Are you sure about that? You are watching the television with bated breath. You look scared."

"Well, I..." Jody bit her lip. "I had a friend in Milo's gang. He wasn't like them. He was nice."

Not just nice. She had fallen in love with him, a criminal.

For nearly two years, she had taken car rides with him and chatted about her life's goals and her innermost thoughts. She had looked forward to seeing him every day. She had been conflicted. She had always looked down on the women in her neighborhood who willingly paired up with gangsters and became a part of their little harem without blinking an eye.

And yet, she hadn't been able to stop herself from growing

emotionally attached to King, a man who had been an integral part of Milo's gang, a man who had lived with his girlfriend.

To King's credit, he had never once made a move on her, but would she have resisted if he had?

She didn't know if she would. She had eagerly taken this job at Monroe Ministries, not only to escape Black Lane but to escape her memories of King.

"So where is he, your nice... er, friend?" Tawny asked.

"I don't know," Jody murmured. "Probably in hiding like so many of Milo's henchmen. The community was still under heavy police and soldier surveillance, and every other day you hear on the news that an associate of Milo's was captured."

She always tensed herself up to hear if any of them was King. Why had she mentioned any of it to her boss she couldn't say?

To her credit, Tawny did not seem fazed by her confession. "You can't help who you love," Tawny shrugged.

They had moved on, or so she had thought. But Tawny had filed it away in her brain and was using it to buy her silence about what she had heard and seen Thursday night. She was promptly drawn back to the present when the policewoman at the door looked at her skeptically.

"Did you hear what I just asked?"

Jody shook her head. "I am sorry, I didn't hear. I was stunned for a minute there. You said Bishop Nathan is dead?"

The policewoman nodded, "and his sister Lydia."

"Yes, of course," Jody swallowed. "That's why there are so many people milling around."

"Did you hear or see anything last night?" the policewoman asked.

"No... er," Jody swallowed. She sounded guilty even to her own ears.

The policewoman picked up on it and narrowed her gaze. "Are you sure about that?"

"Well," Jody swallowed, "the bishop stopped here last night. He said he wanted to talk, clear the air. We had... er, we had a situation at his mother's office, and he... he wanted to apologize and tell me his side, I guess..."

"What situation?" the policewoman asked.

"He said something he shouldn't have. It wasn't intentional. He came to apologize last night. I am his mother's secretary, Jody Fyre." She was tripping over her words.

She felt like such a liar, and yet she wasn't lying. She just couldn't give details.

The policewoman nodded, jotted down notes, and then nodded at her. "We'll keep in touch."

Jody closed the door. Oh, please don't, she thought.

She had planned to go to the church for the much-touted musical extravaganza that had been advertised for months, but she would miss that. She was going to sleep, and when she woke up, she would find something to eat and then pretend that she had not seen or heard a thing and that the last couple of days hadn't happened.

****

Ice could not wait to knock on Jody's door. He needed to see her face again, hear her voice, and watch her expressions as she articulated a point. Even in his capacity as John Shepherd, undercover pastor, he could not quell his eagerness to be in her sphere again despite her topping his list of suspects.

He was holding out hope that she hadn't eaten yet. He had

gotten enough of her favorite Chinese takeout dishes to feed four. He had also stocked up on ice cream and her favorite cream-filled donuts from a nearby bakery, which he knew for a fact that she could not resist.

He had come prepared to disarm with food. He clearly remembered that Jody could get quite loose tongued when she had pastries in front of her.

It was a bit late on a Sunday to be asking someone for a meal, though. He wasn't sure what his reception would be like.

He knocked on her door. It was beside his apartment.

She dragged open the door. Her eyes were puffy and a little sleepy, but it was the same beautiful woman he had befriended when he had been undercover the last time. He felt like hugging her to him and confessing that he had missed her.

He just about restrained himself when she blinked at him owlishly, like she needed to clear her vision.

"Er...hello," she cleared her throat.

"Hey," he smiled. "I am your new neighbor; Pastor John Shepherd is the name. I finally found a neighbor who answers."

"Pastor John Shepherd?" She squinted at him. "I didn't know I was getting a new neighbor. Where's Maxine?"

"The previous tenant?" He raised an eyebrow. "I have no clue."

Jody straightened up and ran her hand over her face. "I feel woozy. I hate sleeping during the day. What time is it?"

"After four," he said, rocking back on his heels, pushing his hand in his pocket.

Her belly rumbled loudly. He heard it and smiled. He would need no excuse to convince her to eat.

"Where's everybody?" he asked, confused. "I got enough

food for at least four people, and I was hoping to make some fast friends."

"Everybody is probably at the church. They are having a musical extravaganza today. Some big-name artists are over there."

"I see," Ice nodded. He knew about the extravaganza. He hadn't knocked on any other door. "Would you like to share a meal with me? We have quite a bit of food to go through. I would really like some help."

Jody opened her mouth to refuse, and then her belly rumbled again. "This is so embarrassing."

"It's a natural response to hunger," he interjected, chuckling softly. "No need to be embarrassed. Our bodies have their own way of letting us know when it's time to refuel."

Jody nodded, a hint of a smile tugging the corners of her mouth. "Who did you say you were again?"

"Pastor John Shepherd, grief and trauma counselor," he introduced himself. "I am supposed to start working tomorrow over at Monroe Ministries."

"Oh," Jody nodded. "There was talk of having a permanent staff counselor."

"That's me," John nodded. "Are you coming by to help me with this food or what?"

"Give me five minutes," her belly rumbled again. "Make that three. I am going to freshen up."

"Okay," he smiled. "I am right next door."

Jody stared at him and frowned. "Your smile looks familiar."

Ice raised an eyebrow. "It does?"

"Yes," Jody shook her head. "Don't mind me. Maybe my hunger is making me hallucinate."

"What's your name again?" Ice asked, trying to throw her off his scent. He couldn't believe it only took a smile for her to figure out who he was.

"Jody Fyre," she smiled.

"I like it," he nodded. "Fyre is a nice surname."

Jody nodded and took a step back. It wasn't just his smile; it was his voice too. There was a certain timber to it that reminded her of King. Though Pastor Shepherd sounded much more refined than King ever had.

But it couldn't be King. Maybe she was in a dream, and this was her fantasy version of King. She had always fantasized about seeing him again, and he would magically morph into a law-abiding citizen with a regular job. They would meet, get married, have kids, and live a normal life away from the ghetto.

Jody splashed some cold water on her face and slapped her cheeks. "Wake up, Jody. This is no dream. You are awake. King did not appear at your door, looking like a handsome pastor. Stop the fantasy."

Chapter Six

Pastor Shepherd's apartment was the same as hers—open concept, one bedroom with a spacious living area seamlessly flowing into a small kitchen. The walls were painted beige, while hers was light grey.

Sunlight streamed through the patio doors, and a gentle breeze wafted through the space.

He had laid out the food on the dining room table in their containers, and he hadn't been joking when he said he had enough food for four.

What had taken her aback was that he had all her favorite Chinese food on display. It was as if he could read her mind. There was General Tso's chicken—the crispy chicken chunks coated in a sweet and slightly spicy sauce with a hint of tanginess. It made her mouth water just looking at it. King had introduced her to that dish. Her previous favorites had been Kung Pao Chicken and Ma Po Tofu. They were all there, including the hot and sour soup she had not had since her last meal with King.

He had turned to her with the bowl of soup in hand and had said, "If food is a love language, then we're fluent in it." His eyes twinkled with warmth as he touched his bowl to hers. That had been their thing—doing a cheer with their soup.

"Everything okay?" Pastor Shepherd asked, pulling out a chair for her to sit. "You had a faraway look in your eyes for a moment there. I hope all the food I bought was up to your standards."

"It is," Jody nodded. "I was baffled that you have all my favorites."

He smiled. "Well, then, we have something in common because all of them are my favorites. I am happy that you were around when I knocked on your door. Maybe we should explore what else we have in common, Miss Fyre."

Jody smiled. "I would like that."

"I also have dessert," he said. "Nothing fancy, just some cream-filled donuts and chocolate ganache ice cream because it is Sunday."

"Are you serious?" Jody asked excitedly. "You are not putting me on?"

"Is that something else that you like?" he asked cautiously.

"Yes!" Jody squealed. "Down to my favorite ice cream flavor of all time. Chocolate ice cream is boring, but chocolate ganache is something else."

"I am truly in awe," he said, "and more than a little intrigued that our tastes are so closely aligned."

Jody had to prevent herself from scarfing down the food like a starving animal.

She slowed down when she caught Pastor Shepherd looking at her indulgently. "I am so sorry," she said after a while. "This is a lifesaver. I didn't have breakfast."

"Don't worry about it," he said dismissively. "If you are hungry, eat."

His phone rang; the ringtone was the soundtrack from 'A Song of Ice and Fire.' She recognized it instantly because she was a Game of Thrones fan—the books, not the movies. That was one of the things she had in common with King; he loved to read. She had lent him her collection of George RR Martin's books, beginning with A Game of Thrones. He had found the series name fascinating for some reason, and he hadn't given her back her books.

She listened to Pastor Shepherd's one-sided conversation. She couldn't wait to ask him about his ringtone.

"So sorry, Mom," he said regretfully. "I had to leave; I started my new job early this morning."

"Yes, I heard about the Monroe murders, and yes, I am just as shocked as you are."

He looked at Jody and smiled. "I will call you back later. I have company."

His mother said something, and he burst out laughing.

"Yes, she's female, and no, she doesn't know that I am single and a fine young man yet. I just met her. You have to give me a chance to at least converse with her. Love you too, Mom. You can tell me the latest juicy family gossip later. I'll call you."

He hung up the phone and laughed.

Jody smiled. "You are close to your mom?"

"Yes," Ice nodded, "I am her baby, the only boy, the third of three."

"Oh," Jody smiled. "Close-knit family?"

"Very," Ice chuckled. "I am the only one living in Jamaica. My mom comes out every six months and stays with her sister—she's a retired mental health nurse. My father is a lawyer with his own firm and has no intention of retiring.

Both my sisters are happily married."

"Oh, that sounds lovely," Jody said. "How long have you been a pastor?"

He hesitated before answering. "I like to think of myself as more of a counselor."

"Oh yes, that's your chief role here," Jody cleaned her plate.

Ice started removing the containers. "Would you like some leftovers? I have enough for a couple of days."

"Yes, please," Jody nodded.

He brought out the desserts. They were from the bakery she liked, and the ice cream was the brand she loved. He was either a mind reader, or they had met somewhere before. This was more than a mere coincidence.

"Are you a Game of Thrones fan?" she asked him when he sat down.

"Yes," he nodded. "What gave me away? The ringtone on my phone?"

"Yes," Jody nodded. "I recognized the ice and fire tune."

He smiled. "I love the name combination and the message of using the two. Ice is often associated with coldness, rigidity, and logic, while fire symbolizes passion, intensity, and change. When these contrasting elements come together, it creates a powerful dichotomy that resonates deeply with me."

Jody nodded enthusiastically. "I agree. I have not met anyone who has read the books so we can discuss them. I am so excited about this."

Ice smiled. "Well, I am here. I read widely, and when I say wide, I even like romances. I have heard that only ladies read romances, but my mother had a bookcase full of them, and one summer, I was bored and read them all. Can I tell you a secret, Jody?"

"Yes," Jody nodded solemnly.

"I have written several books, but I haven't shared them with anyone as yet. They are just sitting on my computer."

"Really?" Jody whispered. "What are they about?"

"Detective-based, with some romance and suspense thrown in. I am a closet author."

Jody chuckled. "I can be your first reader. I'll tell you if they are any good."

"I'll consider it," Ice said, "when I come out of the closet."

"You remind me of someone," Jody said. "He was well-read too. He liked Plato, Socrates, and Aristotle. I never could understand why."

"They were influential Greek philosophers," Ice said. "I had to study their writings in Bible school, as they lined up with the Apostle Paul's writings. Paul quoted them a lot."

"Is that so?" Jody breathed. "I didn't know that."

"What's your friend's name?" Ice asked. "Was he a pastor too?"

"I don't know his full name," Jody frowned. "And he never gave me much personal information about himself. He was a gangster. He said it was for my safety that I didn't know too much about him. His name was King. I probably shouldn't be mentioning him. I just... you remind me so much of him. It's not really your looks per se or your mannerisms. I can't put it into words."

"A gangster," Ice raised his eyebrows, "who reads Plato and Aristotle? Why?"

"I don't know. Maybe I am reaching," Jody frowned. "I am baffled as to how you know so much about me."

"I do? How?" Ice took a spoonful of his ice cream and ate it slowly.

"Well, the food, the 'Ice and Fire' song, the Game of Thrones... forget it," she laughed self-consciously when she saw Pastor Shepherd's rapidly ascending brows. "I know I sound a bit off. I had a rough couple of days. And last night was quite the night."

"From your perspective, what happened last night?" Ice asked. "Do you know exactly what happened? I am getting a little feedback here and there. And I'm sure I will be briefed tomorrow. What a time to report to work, huh?"

"To tell you the truth, I'm still having problems coming to grips with the fact that Bishop Nathan and Miss Lydia are gone," Jody said. "I was talking to him last night. Death is strange—one minute you are here, and the next you are gone."

"Ah, so you saw him last night?" Ice leaned back in his chair and regarded her intently.

"Yes, I did," Jody nodded. "He came over to apologize for something I saw on Thursday. The next thing I know, they are both dead."

She opened her mouth to say more and then closed it. "Never mind."

"No, talk to me," Ice urged her silently. "What was it, may I ask?" he said out loud.

Jody shook her head. "It's just..."

"Does it have anything to do with his death?" Ice leaned forward. He didn't know what he was expecting. It wasn't a confession, but she obviously knew something.

"I don't know," Jody said. "I don't know what to think anymore. On Thursday, I saw… I heard..."

Her voice petered out, and she swallowed.

What? Ice wanted to ask. If he could drag the words out of her mouth, he would.

"The longest time I have ever spoken to Bishop Nathan was last night," Jody continued. "He isn't the bad guy everyone makes him out to be. He is somewhat misunderstood."

"He is?" Ice leaned forward. "In what way?"

"It is assumed that he has an affair with all the women who work for his mother," Jody explained. "When I came here, they were warning me about him. On my first day in the lobby, on my way to the interview, Bishop Stevens warned me off from Bishop Nathan without knowing me and knowing what I stood for. In my interview with Mrs. Monroe, one of the three questions she asked me was if I dated married men? For a church-based organization, I thought it was all crazy."

Ice nodded. "It does sound off."

"Bishop Nathan said none of the rumors were true," Jody continued. "He was friendly and cordial to all women. He may flirt a bit, but... all I can say is he has never made a pass at me personally, so I believe him."

Jody lowered her voice. "He said he thinks his mother is the one who started the rumors."

"Say it isn't so," Ice frowned. "Why would she do that?"

"I don't know," Jody sighed. "I heard and saw things on Thursday. Next thing I know, she is firing me on Friday because I know too much."

"What do you know?" Ice asked, intrigued.

Jody sighed. "Sorry, I shouldn't have said a thing. I was promised a glowing recommendation for my next job, If I keep my mouth shut."

"I see," Ice looked at her intently. "But if you tell me, I can't tell anyone else. Rest assured, Jody, your secret is safe with me. As a professional, I understand the importance of maintaining confidentiality. You can confide in me without any fear of it being shared."

"I am just going to keep my head down, and then I'll be out of here in a month," Jody changed the topic. "Which church were you at before you came here?"

"Happy Vale Tabernacle," Ice said. It was what was on his character profile. His origin story that he hadn't even memorized yet.

"Happy Vale? Never heard of it," Jody shrugged. "Then again, I haven't been to many places. My grandmother's family is from Westmoreland."

"The other end of the island," Ice smiled, pretending he hadn't heard this before. She used to tell him about her summers in Westmoreland and the fun she had with her cousins and other relatives.

"My grandmother worked as a practical nurse at the Kingston Public Hospital for many years. She is retiring soon and returning to Westmoreland to be close to her daughters and other grandkids. She had five children, two boys and three girls. One of the two boys was my father."

"How did he die?" Ice asked.

"Gun violence, bad living. Both my dad and uncle were in gangs."

"Oh," Ice said, pretending this was the first time he heard her story.

"My grandmother has always wanted to return to the country," Jody said wistfully. "Since I lost my job, I might have to go with her because she is selling the house. In fact, it's already sold. I have no job, so how will I afford rent anywhere? All of this is unfair."

"I'll help you find another job if you want. As for a place to live, I have a friend who recently bought a townhouse. It's new and in one of those gated communities where they do a background check before you can purchase a place."

"I can't afford a place like that," Jody widened her eyes.

Ice chuckled. "I think he would pay you to stay there. He is hardly there and doesn't want it to just sit around. He was considering renting the place as an Airbnb and having a property management company deal with it, but he hasn't gotten around to it yet."

"Oh, thank you, Pastor Shepherd," Jody said, her eyes wide. "I can scarcely believe this."

"It's no problem," Ice shrugged.

****

Long after Jody left, Ice lay on the bed and stared at the ceiling. Shadows from a banana tree on the small patio danced in the half-light. He thought about when they first met, how aware he had been of her and how they had become fast friends. He thought of how she had liked him even though he was, by all intents and purposes, a gangster.

It was as if she had gotten him on a cellular level as if his disguise while masquerading as King was just cosmetic, and she could see the real thing. No wonder she was confused today. She could sense him deep within.

The awareness had been there from the moment they had locked eyes after he knocked on her door. She knew him. That was reassuring; she hadn't forgotten. What he felt wasn't one-sided.

Some people called what they had a soul connection. This bond surpassed the boundaries of time and circumstance, transcending the labels and masks they wore in their respective lives. Ice couldn't help but wonder if their meeting again was simply a stroke of serendipity or a sign from God that their paths were meant to intertwine.

He had been more outgoing with her today, letting her into his real life like he couldn't before. Letting her see him talk to his mother, telling her information about his real family background, telling her about his writing.

He had let her in.

He wanted this time to be the last time he was undercover with Jody. He wanted a real relationship with her after this. He had bought the townhouse two months ago with her and her grandmother in mind. He had wanted them out of Black Lane.

He had been working out how to approach her and convince her without revealing that he was King, without blowing his cover and then this whole situation brought them closer together. Hopefully, it would all work out perfectly.

His ringing phone jolted him out of his contemplations about Jody.

"Just checking in," Chanelle said when he answered. "I just found out something interesting. I don't know if this is even a factor in the case, but Benjamin Monroe is not Tawny Monroe's biological son. His mother is actually Tawny's twin sister Avery who died in childbirth.

"Tawny and Cassius got married months after he was born. Then they had Nathan together a year later, and then the twins, Aaron and Amos, two years later.

"The couple only had three children," Chanelle said.

"No," Ice said, "they have Lydia."

"No, they didn't," Chanelle replied. "I'm looking at Lydia's original birth certificate and her certificate of adoption."

"Say what?" Ice sat up in bed, surprised by the revelation.

"I wonder if they knew they weren't biologically related," Chanelle mused. "And that's why it wasn't that big of a deal to have a sexual relationship. Maybe they were determined to be together and were stopped by their parents."

"Or maybe they didn't know and didn't care and were just determined to be together," Ice murmured. "Either way, it's interesting."

"Either way, it would be a scandal of mega proportions if their relationship got out, especially because their family is selling a perfect family life to the public. And they had to be stopped."

"Wow," Ice murmured, contemplating the implications. "I hadn't considered that angle."

"Someone in that family wanted them gone. You can't rule out Cassius, even though he was the one who came to us," Chanelle continued. "I am cross-referencing all the legal firearm holders who work at the church and live on the compound. It's taking a little time. The ballistic reports will be out on Tuesday."

"In the meantime, I will find out who regularly does target practice because they were both hit in the forehead, execution-style. We were examining the pictures."

"Someone could have hired a hitman," Ice suggested.

"That's true," Chanelle sighed. "Anyway, I am asking Linton to allow you to go and check out the crime scene. And I am sending over the pictures to your company account. You have your work cut out for you."

"And so do you," Ice acknowledged. "Our team is dealing with a lot of cases at the moment."

"And that is why Max is hiring an Operations Coordinator," Chanelle said. "We are actively interviewing people this week."

"Cool," Ice murmured. "I know someone who would like a job. I'll have her send over her resume."

"Fine," Chanelle agreed. "Be careful out there."

"You too," Ice replied, hanging up the phone and smiling at the ceiling. He loved a challenge.

Chapter Seven

Cassius was sitting in the kitchen with Benjamin the morning after the murders. Cassius was grateful for his presence because he felt so numb. He hardly tasted his favorite cereal in front of him. He didn't know that he would have to bury any of his children. It was a burdensome contemplation.

The closest word to describe how he felt was gutted. It was just dawning on him that he had lost both Nathan and Lydia at the same time; two out of five children in the blink of an eye. Yesterday he was all for justice being served swiftly and lethally. Today, he was just bereft and empty. No amount of justice would bring them back.

Tawny entered the kitchen, dressed in her usual power suit, her hair in a chignon, and she had on her pearls. Her power pearls, the black ones she wore when she was in serious first lady mode. They hadn't spoken much yesterday. She had sobbed on and off for most of the day.

"Where are you going?" Cassius asked Tawny incredulously.

"I am going to work," Tawny said. "I have a speech to give at a girls' home in an hour."

"Wow, Mom," Benjamin was stunned. "Nathan and Lydia just died."

"And life continues," Tawny said dryly. "I made this commitment months ago and will fulfill my obligations. That's what your father said when he went to the concert last night, and he will work today. Why does everybody expect me to curl up in a ball and cry for the whole week? I have already shed my tears and will undoubtedly shed more. I can't be sitting in one place, staring out into space. That won't bring them back."

Cassius nodded. "I hear you, Tawny, but we couldn't cancel the concert. It involved a lot of planning, and tickets were already purchased. The artists were already here, and the show had to go on. What you are doing now can be easily canceled. People would understand. You are supposed to be grieving your children who were brutally murdered just yesterday!"

Benjamin cleared his throat and said delicately, "You care about what people say. And I think you are not acting like a grieving mother who just lost two children."

Tawny poured some coffee and looked at her husband and Benjamin stonily. "How dare you tell me how to grieve? Oh, I grieve. I grieve in ways you know nothing about. I grieve about things you are not privy to. I ask myself, why couldn't Lydia and Nathan accept that we are a family and forget about their unnatural love for each other? He was planning to run away with her. He came to my office Thursday. He said to me, 'Mom, I am divorcing Terry, and I am leaving with Lydia where no one knows us, and we are going to start a life away from here. '"

"Wow," Benjamin murmured. "Ballsy."

Cassius didn't move. "Really?"

"And I laughed," Tawny growled. "I laughed. I called him an idiot. Told him he would destroy this family. And you know what that ungrateful man said to me, his mother? He didn't care how things looked anymore. He only cared about how it feels. And he loved Lydia and no one else. In essence, he said he was ready to throw everything away—his career, home, life—and he didn't care if she was his sister."

Tawny teared up. "And I told him the joke's on you, Nathan, because Lydia is adopted. She is a distant relative of your father's. There was no need to run around thinking you were having an incestuous relationship. He lost it. I had never seen him so angry. He called me names. He said he could have avoided all of the drama. He said I was the one who made him marry Terry. He said he hated me."

"Me! I am the glue holding this family and our ministry together. I am the reason he even has a job! I made all of this happen!" Tawny exclaimed.

Cassius grunted. She was right. If it were up to him, he would be the pastor of a humble country church somewhere near the sea. "So, you finally told him the truth? And he hated you for it."

"Hold up, wait a minute," Benjamin frowned. "Lydia was not our sister?"

"She was," Tawny said. "She was officially adopted by us, which means she was your sister."

"I meant biologically," Benjamin said. "What's wrong with you people? That's not a secret you should keep from the rest of your children. At least you could have said something when we were adults."

"Don't look at me," Cassius said. "Tawny was the one

who insisted on her perfect family storyline."

"But you didn't have to go along with it," Benjamin looked between his parents incredulously. "I don't know how to feel right now. I am in my forties and just finding this out. What about Maci Graham? Is she my sister for real? Everybody talks about it, how she resembles you, Dad. Are you and Mariam Graham having an affair?"

"Good Lord, no," Cassius said. "Mariam used to work with your uncle Simon as his secretary. She came to us pregnant with Maci. I think you can connect the dots. Simon refuses to acknowledge that girl, so I make up for her rejection in my own way."

"This family," Benjamin breathed.

"And while we are letting all the gremlins out of the closet," Cassius cleared his throat.

"No," Tawny stepped toward Cassius, "don't you dare say another word."

Cassius ignored her. "Tawny is not your mother. Her twin sister, Avery, was. Avery died in childbirth. I married Tawny a year later. It was more out of convenience than anything else, and here we are."

"A convenience!" Tawny glared at him.

"It was not the great romantic story you made it out to be," Cassius muttered. "Sometimes I wonder who you write about in your little stories."

Benjamin looked between the two of them. "Well, thank you for finally telling me. Grandma told me years ago when I asked her why Mom dislikes me. She told me your whole story."

"What are you talking about, Benjamin?" Tawny said hoarsely. "I do like you. I love you."

"No, you don't," Benjamin said. "And if you do, you have a strange way of showing it. I mean, it's obvious to everyone from the outside looking in that you are cold as ice with me. I accepted it. I told my wife and kids that you are not my mother, and they've accepted it too. Haven't you ever wondered why your grandchildren don't like being around you?"

"I just thought they were well-behaved little ones," Tawny sighed. "As for you, you hated me as a baby. I could not bond with you. I tried everything. It's as if you instinctively knew I wasn't your mother, even though I look just like her."

"I don't think it's that," Benjamin said. "I think you are not very motherly. Children can sense it."

"Cassius, are you going to sit there and let this boy continue to hurt me?" Tawny turned to him dramatically.

Cassius sighed. "I agree with him to a certain extent, Tawny. You are not very motherly. You should own it and stop writing phony books about perfect families and bragging about what a great mother you are. We are not perfect. Our history together is a made-up lie. My children could have had a different outcome if we didn't do so much pretending!"

"I feel like saying amen," Benjamin grunted.

"I won't stay here and be insulted," Tawny said. "I am going to give my speech."

"Maybe some friendly reporter will see things your way," Benjamin said. "They'll say how brave you are for coming out though your children were killed in a gruesome crime. I hope you don't smile too much for the photos."

"Say what you want about me," Tawny growled, "but I fixed things for you, Benjamin. I made your life easier. Remember Claudia, the mentally impaired girl you used to fool around with? Well, when you impregnated her, I was going to take your child and bring her up as our own."

Benjamin swallowed. "Nathan fooled around with her

too! Don't be blaming this on me alone!"

"You are so pathetic blaming this on Nathan when he can't defend himself," Tawny said. "I keep tabs on that child. Her name is Mercedes Nelson. She is yours! Would a cold, unfeeling mother keep up with your youthful mistake if I didn't care? Think about that while you mock me. As I said, I grieve in my own way!"

She stormed out of the house.

Cassius looked at Benjamin. "I am going to work. I have a grief counselor to speak to this morning."

"Okay, Dad," Benjamin said contemplatively. "I head back to Montego Bay this evening. Are you sure you are up to going into the office today?"

"I am not sure," Cassius said, "but I have to see this counselor. How is it going with the new job?"

"It's going okay," Benjamin said. "I saw a girl last night at a Mental Health gala. She was there with Charles."

"Dr. Charles Payne," Cassius leaned back in his chair. "I miss that boy as a son-in-law. I am happy to hear he has moved on. I will always have love for him. I wish Lydia had more sense than to lose that man. She probably would be alive now if she had behaved properly in her marriage."

"I agree," Benjamin nodded. "It was nice seeing Charles looking happy. My issue is with his girlfriend."

"What about her?" Cassius asked.

"She looks a lot, and I mean a lot, like Claudia," Benjamin sighed. "And her name is Mercedes Nelson. I didn't even know Mom kept tabs on her."

"Now look at that," Cassius whistled. "You found your daughter."

"I don't know if she is mine," Benjamin shrugged. "She could very well be Nathan's."

"Well, find out," Cassius stood up. "We are losing family

members left, right, and center. It would be nice to gain some."

Chapter Eight

Jody was late getting ready for work. She had thought about Pastor Shepherd all night. It had gotten so bad she was blending him and King in her head.

The two men were so different, it was laughable. So what she was doing was strange. She got into the shower.

No doubt she would have to field a million and one calls today and handle everything, all the inquiries to do with the death of Pastor Nathan and Lydia. It was going to be a hectic day.

And worst of all, she had to start her job hunt and review her resume. She should be focusing on that instead of Pastor Shepherd.

It was the first time since King that she had found a man so fascinating. What did this mean? Had she finally gotten over King? Had it finally registered in her brain that it wouldn't have worked anyway? Why was that man lodged in her brain so conclusively? Maybe the fact that John Shepherd reminded her of King was a sign that she should move on. God knows she wanted to move on. She closed her eyes and remembered.

Sometime in the past...

"I don't like you coming in after dark," her grandmother said. Enid Hutchins had lost two sons to gang violence. And she lived in the middle of Black Lane, so she knew what she was talking about.

"But I have to work late some nights," Jody protested. "If I insist on leaving at five o'clock, I'll lose the job."

"I know you have to work," Enid grunted. "Why don't you go live with your aunties in Westmoreland and work at one of those hotels in Negril?"

Jody had this conversation with her grandmother every other month. She understood why her grandmother was fearful. Black Lane had gotten exponentially worse through the years.

There was a time when it had been a nice community. It was on the outskirts of the hospital and at one time, doctors and nurses lived there.

Her grandmother liked to talk about the days when she bought her three-bedroom house for little or nothing because she had been caring for the owner. He had sold it to her for peanuts; as a young practical nurse owning a home had been a major achievement for her.

She had five children in the interim. Her husband died, and her boys succumbed to the serene call of quick money and fast women.

Jody's father, in particular, got her mother pregnant when they were still in high school. He dropped out of school without any discernible skills and joined a gang. Their relationship didn't last long, and her mother, Amelia, left her with her paternal grandmother and went on to live her life.

Jody didn't remember any of it. She didn't remember any of them. Amelia was shot in a bar she was working when Jody was around three years old, and her father was killed in reprisal for a gang war around the same time.

That was her beginning. And though Black Lane hadn't started as an inner-city community, it had certainly ended up being one.

By the time she had gotten the job with Thelman and Associates, Milo had been running the community.

His style was different; the streets were quieter, and peace reign for a while. He allied with the other dons in the surrounding communities by supplying them with guns and had several law enforcement officials in his back pocket. Under his reign Black Lane was a relatively peaceful place. There were no turf wars. Big celebrities would even party at Dusty's Boudoir, a nightclub owned by Milo and his girlfriend Dusty. Apparently, people started treating Black Lane as an exotic ghetto place you went to when you wanted to know what being in a ghetto was like.

One thing that hadn't changed there was the scant disregard for females. Unlike the other dons elsewhere, Milo did not require people to send their children to him like some sort of tribal overlord in the jungle because he had Dusty, and she was his co-don.

However, he endorsed his various lieutenants keeping whichever girl they wanted from the community. And just like that, there was a new type of crime in Black Lane. Girls who resisted Milo's lieutenants and their families were marked and harassed.

So far, Jody had been spared, mainly because they didn't know she was around. She went outside only if she had to.

Her routine was going to school and returning home, and sometimes church. She never went to any evening services or community events.

She didn't even go to her high school prize-giving ceremony, where she was to collect two awards. She was the embodiment of living in the ghetto but not of the ghetto and so she barely knew any of the other girls there.

She kept to herself, and it had worked up until now.

It was her 21st birthday. Miss Thelman had thrown her a party that continued into the late evening. Yanique Thelman was the best boss ever and she was a good lawyer too. In all conscience, she could not tell the lady that she didn't want a party in her honor because she didn't want to go home too late.

She was nervous walking home from work with her happy birthday balloon and gifts. Two of Milo's henchmen accosted her as soon as she got off the bus and entered the road.

She knew them. She had seen them walking past her house. One of them was Jason Strathaway.

She knew him from high school. And the other boy was Ricardo. He lived two doors down from her.

She glared at them as they approached her in the half-dusk.

"Who do we have here?" Ricardo licked his lips. "Is this the nurse's granddaughter? Boy, you look so pretty."

"Yup, she is pretty," Jason said. "I think you could totally work at Dusty's Boudoir. You would have all the men flocking to you."

Jody inhaled roughly and clutched her gifts tighter.

"Would you like me to walk you home, pretty lady?" Ricardo asked.

"No, thank you," Jody said abruptly. "I'm quite fine

walking by myself."

"Ah, she's feisty," Jason said. "I remember you from high school, Jody. You were always acting as if you were better than all of us. Do you think you're better than me?"

Jody raised an eyebrow and didn't answer.

"Oh, so you think you are," Jason said. "Well, I work for Milo now. And if I want to I can get you just like that. I can do you right here in the street and no one would blink an eyelid. You understand that girl?"

What he said sent shivers down Jody's spine. She had gone through most of her life without this kind of sexual aggression. She started to panic when Jason forcefully grabbed her hand.

"I think you are going to be my girlfriend."

"You already have two girlfriends," Ricardo said. "I only have one. She's going to be my girlfriend."

She snatched her hand from Jason just when a darkly tinted car drove up, the windows wound down.

The driver was bearded. He wore dark shades, and his hair was in a dreadlock style. "Leave her alone," he said.

Both Jason and Ricardo stepped back. "What's up, boss? I didn't know she was your girl."

"She is," he said. He didn't even crack a smile.

Jody could feel the menace rolling off him. She took a step back as well.

"Get in," he said to her.

Jody had a decision to make. Trust this guy in the car or be potentially raped by two hyenas. She decided to trust the guy in the car.

She went around to the passenger seat.

"Spread the word, she's off-limits," he said.

"Okay, boss," the two guys nodded. "Sure, sure thing, boss."

Jody sat in the passenger seat nervously. She didn't even know what to make of this guy.

He looked over at her. "The name is King. What's your name?"

"Jody, Jody Fyre," she stammered.

"Why have I never seen you around here, Jody Fyre?" he asked.

"Because I grew up not associating myself with anybody here."

"Understandable," King nodded. "Where do you live?"

"Just around the corner," Jody said. "My grandmother is Nurse Enid."

"Ah," King said. "Nurse Enid is well known around these parts." He dropped her off. "Well, have a good evening, Jody Fyre."

"Er," Jody found herself pausing before she left the car. "Thank you so much for rescuing me from those guys."

"Don't worry about it. They won't trouble you again," King said. "No one around here will trouble you again."

Jody grinned. "Okay, then."

"To be on the safe side," King said, "if you want a pickup after work, I can arrange that. Give me your phone."

She handed him her phone, and he punched in his number and entered the name, King.

"Is King your first name or your surname?" Jody asked.

"Just King," he said. "Have a good evening, Jody."

She left the car feeling both relieved and curious.

There had been a spark of attraction when she looked at King. A jolt of awareness between the two of them. She hadn't ever felt that way before. It was new and exciting.

True to his word, nobody troubled her after that. As a matter of fact, walking into the community, the same guys, Jason and Ricardo, actually told her good evening respectfully. They started calling her Miss Jody.

Jody concluded that King was certainly influential, but she didn't want to know too much about that.

One night after a steady downpour, and she was at the office, she called him. "Can you come and get me?" she asked.

"Sure," he replied. "I'm already outside your building."

He exited the car with an umbrella for her, and that's when she realized how tall he was.

"I anticipated your needs, madam," he said respectfully. "That's just the way I roll."

That was the first night they chatted way up into the night. They usually sat in his car at her gate or in the parking lot of the various restaurants, or they drove around and chatted.

They never went out together, attended a party, or did anything. He said he wanted to keep her away from his friends and associates. And she was fine with that.

He had a fascinating view of life. He was intelligent and kind. Almost a year later, she found out that he lived with Misha, one of the girls that worked at Dusty's nightclub. Jody had been devastated. She had tearfully told King she didn't want to talk to him anymore.

"But why?" King asked her. "We're just friends."

That's when she realized she didn't consider King, a friend. She thought of him as her boyfriend. It felt that way. They spent all their evenings together. He picked her up from work. They had something to eat and chatted into the night. They had formed a little book club of sorts, where they discussed the books they were reading.

She went home, and he went his way.

But he had never, not once, tried to touch her or even indicate that he was interested in her. It was a hard pill to swallow. But swallow it, she did.

For an entire year, she kept her fantasies of them being together under wraps until King disappeared.

And now she was feeling the same thing for this pastor. Jody stepped out of the shower. Maybe this time, things could be different. One could only hope. She had never had a real relationship, and it sucked that she was leaving Monroe Ministries just when he arrived. She got ready for work with more anticipation than she had in the past four months.

****

"So we meet again, Jody Fyre," Pastor Shepherd greeted her warmly as she entered the lobby area of the building on Monday morning.

Jody smiled. She had thought about him all morning, and here he was, standing in the lobby. Looking handsome and debonair in his dark grey suit and skinny red tie. His glasses were silver-framed.

He might as well put a sign around his neck marked 'eligible bachelor.' The women in the building were going to go wild over him. She would not stand a chance. Everyone was going to suddenly claim him as an answer to their prayers. Just standing at the elevator, people slowed down to check him out.

Even Maci from HR, who acted like she was better than everyone else, was gawping at him like a fish without water.

He looked at Maci and gave her a wave.

Maci waved back.

"So it starts," Jody murmured.

"What starts?" he asked, staring at her intently.

"The bomb rush for your attention. A single handsome pastor is like red meat among wolves."

He laughed. "If only I hadn't seen you first, they would stand a chance, but I did, so they don't."

Jody smiled.

He punched the button for the seventh floor and looked at her. "Seventh is your floor?"

"Yes," Jody stammered.

"Well, that's where I am headed. First day for me, I need to report to the boss."

"Oh yes," Jody said. "It will probably be a tough meeting."

"I can feel it already," he sighed. "The atmosphere here is solemn. I guess I have my work cut out for me."

They entered the elevator together and stood side by side.

"What time do you take lunch? And do you have your lunch in the cafeteria?"

"Around one o'clock," she replied. "And yes, in the cafeteria."

"Well, see you then," he gave her a little salute as they exited the elevator. "Have a good day today, Jody."

"You too," Jody replied huskily.

Chapter Nine

"**P**astor Shepherd," a well-dressed middle-aged woman in a black suit, greeted him in the lobby on the seventh floor as he was about to go to the receptionist to inquire where his office was. "My name is Mariam Graham, Bishop Monroe's secretary. He asked me to escort you to see him."

Ice grinned. "I feel special. How are you holding up after the tragedy?" he asked Mariam. He was quite interested in her response. Everyone he spoke to today was a suspect, except for Jody. He had ruled her out.

"It's overwhelming," Mariam sniffed. "I keep reminding myself that bad things happen to good people all the time. I never thought it would be at our doorstep and in such a spectacular and tragic fashion. The seventh floor will feel empty without Bishop Nathan, and I will miss Lydia's daily phone calls to her daddy. She was such a sweet young woman, quite a daddy's girl."

"That's why I am here," Ice said gently. "You can talk

about it with me."

"I am happy you are here," Mariam nodded. "We have a little memorial and prayer group meeting scheduled at twelve in the multipurpose hall on the ground floor. Maybe you would like to say something as our new grief counselor."

"I will just listen for the time being," Ice said. "Surely those who knew Lydia and Nathan best would love to speak more than I would."

Mariam smiled. "You are right."

She led him to an office that was nothing short of spectacular. It could rival his father's law firm in New York.

Cassius was at his desk, staring into space.

He barely registered that Ice was there. He finally made eye contact when Ice sat down. "You look exponentially different," were his first words. "I'm not even sure you are one of Saint Wiley's guys. Are you the same man I saw yesterday morning?"

"I am," Ice nodded. "You look different too, like the depression stage of grief has kicked in."

"You may be right," Cassius said listlessly. "I find myself wondering, what is it all for? Who are we going to leave all of this to? Tawny and I worked so hard to build all of this up. Nathan was our legacy. None of the other children care about it like he did."

"Sell it to another mega-church or wait until your grandchildren grow up," Ice shrugged. "Children don't always follow in their parent's footsteps; they tend to take their own path. Your dreams are not their dreams."

"I hear you, and I agree," Cassius sighed. "I am from a family with a business too. My brother Simon followed in our father's footsteps, but I've always wanted to do ministry and help people. I didn't think I was cut out for the business world."

"That's funny," Ice smirked. "So, how did you end up here? A mega-church is a business. Some of you make more money than large corporate operations."

"I know," Cassius sighed. "Believe it or not, this was not my intention. It was Tawny's."

"Your wife?" Ice raised an eyebrow.

"It's Tawny's world; I just live in it," Cassius said sadly. "Would you like to hear a story?"

"Sure," Ice nodded.

Cassius steepled his fingers on the desk. "It's a story about where we are coming from and the family I have now."

Ice nodded. "I am listening."

"When I was eighteen, I fell in love with a girl named Avery, my parents' housekeeper's daughter. She was gentle and kind, a nurturer. I had plans to marry her and have a family; she would be a homemaker. I wanted to attend Bible College and eventually become a pastor, and then we would get a little country church, maybe close to the sea. We both liked the sea," Cassius said wistfully.

"My father had other plans for me though. He sent me to college overseas. I was supposed to study business management and run a part of the family business. We were in shipping. It was expected, no questions asked. It was also expected that I would return home for the summer and work in whatever capacity my father saw fit so that I could gain experience. But I was a poor worker, a disappointment. I preferred to spend all my time with Avery.

"Unfortunately, that fueled my parents' dislike of her. She became known as the girl who was leading me along the wrong path, which couldn't be further from the truth. I got Avery pregnant in the second year of college. My father found out and paid her to disappear. She didn't tell me about any of that; she just broke up with me over the phone. Told me to forget her; she had moved on. I later found out she went to live in Spanish Town with her dad and twin sister Tawny."

"Her twin sister?" Ice asked.

"Yes." Cassius sighed. "Tawny's sister, Avery, was my first love."

"Oh?" Ice replied as if he hadn't heard this just last night. "Wow."

"I was flunking my management course, getting all low grades, two semesters running. My dad said I should come home, stop wasting his money, and do what I wanted to do. He gave me some money and said, 'You are free to go.'"

Ice grinned. "Sounds a lot like my dad."

"It takes a while, but fathers eventually see the light," Cassius said. "I did not make that mistake with any of my sons. Benjamin wanted to do mathematics. He even taught at a high school. I never imposed my vision on him one bit. On the other hand, Nathan would always follow me around and take an interest in the ministry and how it was run. Now he was a natural fit for this place. My other two sons, Amos and Aaron, were science nerds, little geniuses who hated everything religious."

Cassius chuckled. "Amos would drive his mother crazy when she carried him to children's church. He always had a different spin on the Bible stories, and Aaron would ask the teachers difficult questions about angels, aliens, and ancient tech."

Ice chuckled. "So, how did you come to marry Tawny? And where does Benjamin fit into the picture?"

"I saw Tawny in a shopping center. She was pushing a pram with a baby in it who looked like me," Cassius said. "That's when I learned that Avery had died in childbirth, and Tawny was left to care for her twin sister's baby. I married her a few months later, and we became a family."

"That's not how your story reads in Monroe Family Values," Ice said. "I am at chapter one."

"I know," Cassius nodded. "Tawny is very good at marketing. She reinvented us. People like to hear a perfect little story about their first family. We give them that."

"We had three sons together, Nathan and the twins, and when the boys were in their teens, we had this idea to start another church in the Cayman Islands. We spent a lot of time over there."

Ice nodded.

"For two years, we spent most of our time in Cayman, allowing other people to raise our boys when they were at the stage when they could have used our most dedicated attention. So much for family values, huh?"

Ice shrugged. "Cut yourself some slack."

Cassius leaned back in his chair and sighed. "That's where we got Lydia. Tawny convinced one of my distant cousins not to go through with an abortion and promised to take the baby. Eloise promptly handed over Lydia. We officially adopted her, and there, our family was complete."

"It's remarkable. She got the Monroe eyes, and she slightly resembles Tawny. Nobody suspected that she wasn't ours. We didn't tell anyone, not even the boys. They just knew their mommy returned from Cayman with their baby sister," Cassius explained.

Ice raised an eyebrow. "Now that's an unnecessary family secret."

"Tawny didn't want them to treat her differently. She wanted a cohesive family. Everybody assumed that Benjamin was hers, so why not do the same with Lydia?" Cassius replied.

Ice rubbed his neck. "So let me get this straight, Nathan and Lydia re not closely related?"

"No," Cassius confirmed.

"But they thought they were, and still couldn't leave each other alone?" Ice questioned.

"That's right," Cassius nodded.

"That's cold," Ice said, "downright cold. They died thinking they were biological siblings."

"To tell them that secret would be to tell the world," Cassius said, his voice breaking. "We had the family narrative going for so long. Bishop Cassius and his wife Tawny and their five children. They had their daughter Lydia when they thought they had finished having children. Do you know how many books Tawny wrote about being a mother over forty? How many podcasts and television interviews she gave about having a daughter after four sons?"

"It just seems such an inconsequential thing to lie about," Ice said. "Does Benjamin know that he is not her son?"

"He found out from his grandmother, Tawny's mother, when he was younger," Cassius sighed. "I didn't know until this morning that he knew. Nathan and Lydia would still be here if we didn't like to keep up appearances. Nathan genuinely loved Lydia. Maybe if he knew they weren't closely related, they could have had a different story."

Ice listened as Cassius ran through his several maybes. He could almost feel the man's pain from where he sat.

"Maybe we shouldn't have adopted Lydia," Cassius said hoarsely. "We all saw the weird relationship she had with Nathan. If she liked someone, he tried to make her jealous. They both acted possessive and possessed about each other. I honestly thought that when Lydia married Charles, that would be the end of it. I begged God to let them find a way to make peace about their feelings for each other."

"I begged Nathan to leave Lydia alone. He listened for a while, and then he and Lydia ended up back at square one as lovers when both were married. It wasn't right. I talked to him about it, but to no avail," Cassius continued.

Ice cleared his throat. "Maybe he didn't want to listen because he thought you had no moral authority to tell him anything."

"Then he would be wrong. I have never been unfaithful to Tawny. I take my marriage vows seriously," Cassius sniffed. "I know there is a completely unfounded rumor that I am having an affair with my secretary, Mariam, and that her daughter Maci is mine. It is not true. I practice what I preach."

"Maci resembles you," Ice said. "I saw her in the lobby this morning. I did a double take."

"She is the result of an extramarital affair with Mariam and my brother Simon. Mariam used to work at Monroe Shipping when they had their affair. Now that's another family secret I can't clear up even if I wanted to. Simon's wife, Mandy, is mentally fragile. She cannot handle news like this. So I grit my teeth and bear the rumors. Mariam is a good secretary, and it has never crossed my mind to try anything with her."

"Oh," Ice said.

"Speaking of Maci, I want her to be the one to introduce you around," Cassius said huskily. "She was recently promoted to director of human resources. I already directed her to tell the staff in her daily emails that you should be accommodated for grief counseling sessions."

Ice nodded. "That will make my job that much easier. In whose direction should I look first? Do you have any ideas?"

"I don't have the faintest clue. Ask Maci to assist," Cassius said weakly. "I might have to take the rest of the day. I thought I would be up for the office this morning, but I find that I am not."

"Take your time, Bishop," Ice said sympathetically. "I'll find out who killed your children."

Chapter Ten

Maci Graham was definitely a Monroe. She was an attractive, feminine version of Cassius with her almond-shaped eyes, short straight nose, and generous lips. She was dressed impeccably in a dark skirt suit that fit her like a glove.

She met him at the door of Cassius' office and gave him a pleasant smile. "Welcome to Monroe Ministries, Pastor Shepherd."

"Thank you," Ice smiled. He wanted to say more, but she started talking quickly.

"I will just give you a brief rundown of our building," Maci said. "We'll work from the top down."

Ice nodded. "No problem."

"Your office is through here," she pointed to a spacious office two doors down from Cassius'.

"Wow," Ice murmured. "So close to the boss and with a nice view too."

"Well, it was empty since... er, the tragedy. It was Bishop Nathan's office."

"I knew it had to be something like that," Ice said, looking around. "It's nice in here." He looked at the two photo frames that Nathan had on his desk. One was of him and his wife Terry and his two boys. Terry was a pretty woman who had a waif-like look about her as if a good gust of wind could blow her over. Their sons looked like the Monroe side of the family, and the eldest was a miniature Cassius.

"The other photo frame was of Nathan and Lydia. They were smiling at the camera, his hand casually looped around her neck. They looked happy and carefree and in love."

"Where is Nathan's secretary?" he asked.

"Leona is on sick leave for four months. Nathan shares Bishop Gordon's secretary, Phedora. Bishop Gordon is our director of strategic planning. He occupies the office next door."

"Ah, when do I get to meet Phedora?" Ice asked.

"Later, I suppose," Maci looked at him suspiciously. "Your appearance here was quite unexpected. Usually, Bishop Monroe leaves all hiring decisions to HR. You skipped the process altogether."

"He probably considered me to be an urgent need, especially in his time of grief," Ice said.

"And that is what bugs me," Maci narrowed her eyes at him. "I am yet to see your resume or qualifications. You could have fraudulent degrees. I have had to put measures in place because of fraud, as we have been duped before."

"I assure you; my qualifications are up to snuff for this job," Ice said, trying not to smile. Maci looked pissed. Obviously, she did not like being kept out of the loop.

"I go away for one weekend," Maci huffed, "and now this happens."

"Where did you go?" Ice asked. "If you don't mind me prying?"

"Girls' trip to Negril with a few of my friends. It was fun," Maci said. "We wanted a weekend with no distractions. It was only while we were coming back Sunday night that I heard about the murders."

Ice headed for the desk and sat down. The office had a wonderful chair. He needed to find out who they bought their office furniture from and make a recommendation to Wiley Securities.

"Have a seat, Miss Graham," he looked at Maci's scowling face.

"I am supposed to be showing you around," Maci said, sitting before him in the plush guest chairs across from his desk.

"Why don't you give me a general idea where everything is?" Ice said, "And I'll slowly make my way around the building. I heard you already alerted everyone to my presence via email. Let's start from the ground floor up and tell me who, in your opinion, would urgently require a grief counselor."

"Well, okay then," Maci said, a hint of hostility still in her voice. "The basement area of the building houses our underground car park and our maintenance department."

"Maintenance," Ice nodded. "Is there anyone there who you think I should prioritize for a visit?"

"Mario James," Maci said without batting an eyelid. "He should be pretty cut up about this."

"May I ask why?" Ice asked.

"Well, he was Lydia's most recent fling," Maci shrugged. "She is not discriminatory regarding her flings. Mario is an ex-con, one of the many individuals we employ when they are done with our Rehab and Renew program."

"Ex-con?" Ice raised an eyebrow. "What was he in for?"

"Assault and battery, I believe," Maci said patiently. "He was a drug addict, but he is reformed, or we wouldn't have him on staff."

"I will visit Mario James," Ice jotted down the name.

"On the first floor is the main entrance and lobby, where we have the church auditorium. That's where Sunday services are held. We have the community center, the multipurpose hall for events and workshops, the gymnasium, the lounges, and the cafeteria."

"What am I forgetting? Oh, the sound and lighting room and music ministry area. Pastor Mark McGowan heads the music department, he had a soft spot for Lydia. They shared a very strange taste in Gregorian chants. I think they were producing an album together or something."

"Gregorian chants?" Ice raised an eyebrow. "Isn't that a rather unconventional musical preference? I know this church has a contemporary worship style."

"Yes," Maci nodded. "But I must grudgingly admit that Pastor McGowan does put a modern spin on it, enhancing worship."

Ice smiled. "I'll have to listen to that when I visit him. Is there anyone else?"

"We have several prayer rooms on that floor," Maci said. "The prayer coordinator, Sister Evans, has her office there. She loved Nathan. He called her his second mom; she will definitely be grieving."

Ice nodded.

"He was also quite popular with the cafeteria and gift shop staff. There was one particular lady down there, Imogen, who growls at anyone who says anything negative about Nathan, even when he is clearly in the wrong," Maci rolled her eyes.

"You seem to find that disturbing," Ice observed.

"I hate the deification of clergy," Maci said. "They are mere men, and in Nathan's case, not the best example of what we morally stand for in this building. But I guess he is dead now, so I will keep my thoughts to myself."

"Anyway," she quickly said before Ice could inquire what those thoughts were, "the second floor houses the Sunday school classrooms, the children's ministry area, the nursery and toddler rooms, the youth ministry area, and the pastoral offices, which is where you should be, with the rest of our pastoral staff."

Ice grinned. "You have a problem with me being up here, don't you?"

"I do," Maci growled. "I like to do things properly. There are several counseling rooms on the second floor, and we do have pastors on staff with counseling degrees that I have verified. Why are you so special?"

Ice chuckled.

"We also have the administrative offices on that floor, where you would have an assistant," Maci added. "I wish the bishop had not gone over my head."

"I like working alone," Ice said, "and I like it on the seventh floor in this office. Surely, the employees will appreciate that I am located on the seventh floor and, therefore, must be important enough to talk to."

"I don't know about that," Maci sighed. "I will sort this out shortly."

Ice smiled. "Is there anyone on the second floor I should be particularly concerned about?"

"No," Maci said abruptly. "Of the fifteen pastors on staff, I doubt any of them are shedding a tear about Nathan's death. He wasn't well-liked by his fellow clergymen. He was, in effect, their boss, but they disapproved of his lifestyle."

"His lifestyle?" Ice raised a brow. "You should tell me more about that."

"I am not gossiping with you," Maci sniffed.

"It's not gossiping when it will make my job easier. The bishop said you were to help me. I will have to tell him that you are uncooperative."

"Don't do that," Maci sputtered.

"Very well," Ice said. "I hope you can be more forthcoming about Nathan and Lydia and their connections."

"I'll try. We have over three hundred people on staff. I don't know all their connections," Maci glared at him. "This feels more like an interrogation."

Ice chuckled. "Counseling in a situation like this involves a little interrogation."

"That's nonsense." Maci narrowed her eyes at him and was silent for several seconds. "Now I know why you are here."

Ice leaned back in his chair. "What are you talking about?"

"Never mind," Maci said grudgingly. "What were you asking about before?"

She was smart; Ice had to give her that. "I wanted to know who to talk to on the second floor about Nathan or Lydia."

"Bishop Zahir Stevens," Maci said. "He and Lydia were engaged for a short while. When I called him last night, he was crying. He should require counseling today."

"Crying?" Ice asked interestedly.

"He was near inconsolable," Maci sighed. "I had no idea Lydia's death would have hit him so hard."

"I wonder why?" Ice asked.

"Because he was Lydia's fiancé until recently. They broke up when he found out Lydia was sleeping with Nathan."

"Say what?" Ice pretended that he was hearing this for the first time.

"I am the one that told him," Maci said, a satisfied gleam in her eye. "I am Lydia's neighbor, and I see Nathan sneaking in and out of her townhouse most nights or early mornings. At first, it didn't dawn on me that they were sleeping together. I mean, how could it? I don't have a filthy mind. I thought they were the regular brother and sister, and he was probably crashing at his sister's place because he had a disagreement with his wife or something. And then, one morning, I saw them kissing at her front door. It all made sense then."

"That's shocking," Ice said. "It must have been devastating for Bishop Stevens to hear this."

Maci snorted. "Zahir and Lydia broke up four months ago after I told him about her and Nathan. I even took a nifty little picture just in case he wouldn't believe me. He probably would not have ended it with her either, but she started showing interest in Mario from maintenance."

"I took a picture of Mario exiting her townhouse in the early morning, too, and sent it to Nathan and Zahir."

"You did?" Ice raised a brow.

"I did. And they had one hell of a meltdown. They both lost their minds," Maci snorted. "Unfortunately, Nathan's revenge was to start seeing Ziya, Zahir's sister."

"The secretary who killed herself?" Ice murmured.

"That's right," Maci sighed. "And Zahir understandably was crestfallen. A condition it gave me great satisfaction to see him in. He should have left Lydia when he saw her with her own brother. Out of anyone in this building, he had good reason to have both Nathan and Lydia permanently out of his life."

Ice opened his eyes wide, and Maci realized what she had said.

"I am not implying that he killed them," Maci said. "And if you are wondering, I didn't kill them, detective. I was not here. My girl trip is a yearly thing we do. We plan it far in advance."

Ice frowned. "I am Pastor John Shepherd, not detective."

"Whatever," Maci waved him off and continued talking about the layout of the buildings. "The third to sixth floor is for the academic staff and mostly classroom spaces that we rent to a university."

Ice nodded.

"And the seventh floor is where we are at. The presidents, vice presidents, and the various heads of departments have their offices up here. I doubt any of these people are suspects or are grieving, except for the bishop and Lady Tawny. But then again, Lady Tawny has a strange way of showing her sorrow. She is at an event this morning."

"I see," Ice nodded. "Why do you hate Lydia?"

Maci paused before answering. "I don't hate Lydia, or should I say, I didn't hate Lydia. Lydia has always wanted to one-up me for some strange reason. She was obsessed with me. I have no clue why."

"Maybe because you look more like her father than she does," Ice said, watching for her reaction.

"That could be a factor," Maci nodded. "I look like the Monroes because I am Simon Monroe's illegitimate child, and my uncle Cassius treats me like family. He invests in me. I repaid him by doing well in school and working in his business. Lydia resents me for doing well, I guess.

"She moved into the townhouses after her failed marriage because I lived there. She could have lived elsewhere but chose to move beside me."

"She targeted Zahir because we were dating. I guess I was too tame for him. I wouldn't be sleeping with any man before marriage, and I would not compromise. But Lydia, on the other hand, was up for anything. He probably liked that better.

"We broke up because of Lydia. She said she wanted him, she told her mommy and daddy, and they made it happen. The irony is, it was not like he loved her or anything," Maci sneered. "He saw an opportunity to move up to the seventh floor… that spineless coward."

"Which would mean you had a lucky escape," Ice said. "Better to know now than to actually marry him and repent later."

"That's one way of looking at it," Maci shrugged.

"So, who did you think killed them?" Ice asked. He had stopped pretending to be a pastor/counselor. Maci was smarter than he had given her credit for, and she had already suspected his true reason for being there.

"It could be anyone. Lydia was a spoiled brat who had a million and one lovers. It doesn't even shock me that she and Nathan had a sexual relationship. She was screwed up in the head. They both were. Whenever she took on a new lover, he would take on one too. And they'd have this little competition between them. That's how Zahir's sister, Ziya, got caught up in this mess."

"Tell me more about Ziya Stevens," Ice asked.

"She was an idealist, a young woman in her late twenties. She let the attention that Nathan gave her get to her head. Apparently, he told her he would divorce his wife and marry her. The poor thing was so ecstatic. But he only did it because I outed Lydia and Mario. She was conveniently single, desperate, and close to his office. That seems to be a theme with most of Lady Tawny's secretaries. Nathan seems to have a thing with all of his mother's secretaries."

"Including the current one?" Ice asked curiously.

"I would think so. She looks like his type," Maci cleared her throat. "Is that all, Detective?"

"Please don't call me detective," Ice said wearily. "I am Pastor John Shepherd, sent here to counsel and help the grieving."

"Understood," Maci stood up. "For what it's worth, Pastor Shepherd, I hope you get whoever did this and fast because it gives me the creeps thinking that someone in this building or where I live is a murderer."

Chapter Eleven

Ice slipped into the back pew of the worship room where the memorial service was being held for Nathan and Lydia. He had visited the persons on the list Maci had suggested, except for Mario James and Bishop Zahir Stevens.

He had heard that he could find both men here. It was a great opportunity to observe them from afar.

He spotted Mario immediately. He was still in his coveralls with his name tag on. He was sitting in the opposite aisle, his hands clasped under his chin. He looked sad and bereft, sadder than anyone he had seen today. His face was like an open book; he was wearing his emotions on his sleeve. Mario's eyes appeared heavy with sorrow and fatigue. He was one troubled man.

Ice's major takeaway from his visits today was that people were more shocked than sorrowful. The grief hadn't sunk in yet, and maybe it never would. Genuine grief depended on how close one was to the person who had passed away. Not many people here were genuinely close to Nathan or Lydia. The pro-Nathan people said he was a fun and loving person who did his job exceptionally well, and they would always remember him fondly.

He told them that he was on the seventh floor if they wanted to talk some more. They could call him directly and make an appointment. Everybody nodded politely. He didn't expect to see any of them. As one lady pointed out, she was still traumatized by Ziya taking her life and wanted to know if she could see him about that?

"Sure," he had replied.

He spent the longest time with Pastor Mark McGowan. He was a former soldier who had not lost the bearing of his army career. He was in his late thirties and had pictures of his wife and two little girls, all over his office. There was one photo he found especially fascinating, Mark and his wife were in military dress.

"You and your wife were in the army together?" He asked.

"Yes," Mark nodded. "That's where we met."

"Interesting," Ice smiled, "I went through army training and one of the commandos was female. She was ten times worse than the men."

Mark laughed. "Francesca said it's because they have more to prove."

"Francesca," Ice smiled. "I like that name. Where is she now? "

"Over at the town house, she is on maternity leave, we just had our third child, another girl."

"Congrats man." Ice said.

"Thank you," Mark inhaled and looked down at his hands. "It saddens me that Lydia won't be around for this one. She loved my kids. Lydia and I had a genuine friendship; she was my children's godmother," he said sadly. "I will miss her dearly. She was so creative and talented musically; many people don't know that about her. She helped me out a lot here in the music department."

He played one of her favorite songs with chants, and Ice had to sit and suffer through it. He could understand why he would miss Lydia. Who else could appreciate that music?

He looked around; there were not many staff at the memorial. Maybe because it was near lunchtime? Or was the announcement sent out too late in the day?

Mariam stood up. "This is not the official memorial. I thought that those of us who were close to Nathan and Lydia, who wanted to make sense of their senseless deaths, could pray together and encourage each other. And if you want to say some words about them, that would be nice too. It's good to talk when there is a tragedy. It helps make sense of things."

"And, of course, you can go to Pastor John Shepherd, our grief counselor," she pointed to Ice. "He is here just for us at this time."

Ice waved. The people turned toward him, some nodding warmly. Notably, Mario did not move his head to see who he was.

"We have only half an hour," Mariam said. "I am sure some of you will want to get some lunch. Who wants to say something first?"

"I do." A man in his early to mid-thirties stood up. He was tall, lanky, and good-looking. He didn't have an ounce of spare fat on him. He looked like a long-distance runner.

He cleared his throat and began speaking.

"Thank you, Mariam, for organizing this gathering. Nathan and Lydia were dear friends of mine, and their sudden departure has left a void in my heart."

Ice sat up straighter. Was this really Bishop Zahir Stevens,

Lydia's ex? The man whose sister killed herself over Nathan?

He asked the lady closest to him to make sure.

She nodded and moved even closer to him. "I wrote the speech. Tell me if you like it."

"Nathan and Lydia were incredible individuals, full of life, love, and kindness. With his infectious laughter and unwavering optimism, Nathan always had a way of brightening up any room he entered. On the other hand, Lydia possessed a remarkable strength and compassion that touched the lives of everyone she encountered."

Zahir dramatically paused for a moment.

The room remained silent, attentively listening to his heartfelt words.

"I remember the countless moments we shared together—laughter-filled dinners, deep conversations, and even when we comforted each other during difficult moments. Nathan and Lydia taught me the importance of cherishing every moment and finding joy, even in the simplest things. They showed me what it means to live with purpose and to embrace the beauty of human connection."

His voice quivered slightly as he continued, "Their sudden departure is a painful reminder that life is fragile and unpredictable. But in this moment of grief and confusion, let us come together to find solace and strength in each other. Let us remember Nathan and Lydia not only for their lives but also for their impact on each of us."

"Bravo," Ice glanced at the author.

"Thank you," she preened. "My name is Marissa. I am Bishop Stevens' secretary."

"Well, lovely to meet you, Marissa," he whispered. "You have a knack for writing speeches. Your boss is certainly the actor."

"You think so?" Marissa pursed her lips disapprovingly.

"I told him to put more emotion into it when I heard his first read-through. He could have done a bit better. Maybe in the bigger assembly, he'll put in more emotions."

Ice resisted the urge to laugh. Marissa said it all with a straight face. She was someone he wanted to talk with. She could tell him about Zahir Stevens.

He lost Marissa after the extra-long prayer Mariam offered as they all stood in a circle and held hands.

He wanted to talk to Mario James, and almost missed him.

"Hey Mario," he ran to catch up with his long strides. Mario slowed down and looked at him.

"I don't want counseling, Pastor Shepherd."

"Why not?" Ice asked him. "You looked genuinely sad in there. No one else looked as sad as you."

Mario grimaced. "I will miss Lydia. She was a nice person."

Ice nodded. "When can I see you to talk?"

"I am scheduled to work over at the apartment all week."

"I see," Ice said. "What about this weekend?"

"Fine. Good. If you can find me," Mario said abruptly and sped away.

"A truly unpleasant fellow," Zahir said behind him.

"Oh, he's not that bad," Ice said. "I saw him looking sad and wanted to offer him my services. I am free to all employees, even you."

Zahir laughed heartily. "I did the requisite counseling courses like you did at the seminary."

"I doubt that," Ice said. "I have my master's in the discipline and many years of experience."

"Doesn't matter; I don't want counseling," Zahir shrugged. "I am doing okay."

"Maci said you were distressed last night when she called," Ice said innocently, "and your speech in there almost had me tearing up."

"Maci told you that?" Zahir scowled. "I wasn't handling the news well when I first heard it. I am better now. She caught me at a bad time."

"I see," Ice nodded. "Well, I also heard that Lydia was your fiancée, and when a loved one dies…."

"I didn't love Lydia Monroe," Zahir said. "Please get that straight."

"Got it," Ice nodded.

"And stay away from me," Zahir growled.

Ice stepped back while Zahir stormed away.

His reaction to an innocent offer of help was super interesting. He was going to the top of the suspects list.

****

The cafeteria was enormous. It had an open and spacious layout and could comfortably seat hundreds of individuals. The decor was modern and inviting, with warm earth tones, ample natural light, and tasteful artwork adorning the walls.

The seating arrangements included a mix of long communal tables and smaller, more intimate tables, catering to individuals and larger groups. It reminded him of a hotel dining room.

Ice glanced at his watch. It was near one o'clock and the place was a beehive of activity. Jody was nowhere to be seen. He would take his lunch and wait for her near one of the television sets that was showing a tennis match.

He walked around the several stations. He was spoiled for choice.

The buffet offered a salad bar, soup station, grilled sandwich station, hot entrees with roasted chicken, grilled salmon, pasta primavera, and barbecue ribs. There was also a vegetarian pasta station and a pizza corner with a variety of freshly baked pizzas, including vegetarian and gluten-free options. Lastly, he stopped at the dessert bar. His eyes slithered across the cakes, pies, cookies, and puff pastries.

He was flummoxed.

"Don't be overwhelmed," Marissa said behind him. "You'll get used to it. Every day has a distinct menu. With time you will get the opportunity to try everything. The key is to pace yourself."

Ice smiled.

"Are you vegetarian/vegan or not?"

"Not," Ice said.

"Well then," Marissa said, "my recommendation from the Monday menu is the three-bean soup, the turkey grilled cheese sandwich, roasted chicken with sweet potato gnocchi, pasta salad, and lots of veggies. If you have a sweet tooth, sample all of the pastries."

"Thank you," Ice nodded. "I was overwhelmed for a while there."

"There is Jody!" Marissa waved frantically. "Have you met her?"

"Yes, I have," Ice said. "I was hoping to join her for lunch."

"Sorry, but I am going to be a third wheel," Marissa said unashamedly. "I want a blow-by-blow account of what happened at the apartment Saturday night."

Jody came over to them and smiled at Ice. "I almost didn't make it to lunch. Mrs. Monroe went to a girls' school this morning to give a speech and started crying in the middle of her speech on live television. They had to escort her off the stage. A million and one people have been calling."

"Poor lady," Marissa murmured. "Why did she think she could be giving speeches now? She should be protecting her mental health. Pastor Shepherd is joining us for lunch,"

Marissa turned to Jody.

Jody nodded. "Hello, Pastor Shepherd. Nice to see you again. Such a pity I can't stay long to chat. Mrs. Monroe's office phone is blowing up. I have to log the calls and let her know who showed concern in this time of grief. She makes a note of everyone who calls."

"I understand," he smiled. "It's very good to see you, Jody. I will just get something, and then we'll sit together, okay?"

She nodded. He found himself having to drag his eyes from her face, her precious face. He wished he could tell her who he was, so they could pick up where they left off.

****

"**I** thought the police would be crawling all over the building right now, looking for clues, searching for the criminal," Marissa said after they sat down at a table for four near the dessert station. "This is nothing like the movies."

Ice chuckled. "They do not have the budget like in the movies."

He took a sip of the recommended bean soup and widened his eyes. "This is good. What do they have in this?"

Marissa smiled. "I know, right? You'll be saying that about everything I recommend. I have been here ten years, and in all that time, they rarely mess with the options. I know the ins and outs of the Monday menu."

"The food here is excellent," Jody said. "That's what I will miss about this place, the breakfast and lunch options."

"So it is true?" Marissa wiggled her eyebrows. "Why on earth were you fired? You just got here."

"I saw and heard things I shouldn't have," Jody shrugged.

"Preposterous," Marissa muttered. "I swear that lady has a problem. If she wasn't so phony, people would better appreciate her."

Jody cleared her throat and glanced at Ice.

"Oh, sorry, Pastor Shepherd," Marissa said. "I didn't mean it. Don't tell on me."

Ice chuckled. "I won't tell on you."

"We should take this off campus, so you can tell me what happened," Marissa whispered.

"No." Jody shook her head. "I am trying to forget it ever happened."

"I'm afraid they will not let you forget," Marissa said. "That's why I wanted to have lunch with you today."

"What are you talking about?" Jody asked.

Someone walked near their table, and Marissa said out loud, "The killer could be right out there, right now, walking among us." Marissa looked around. "We can trust no one."

"Sounds like a solid plan," Ice said to Marissa. "Who do you think it is?"

"Mmm, let's see, who would have the motive and opportunity?" Marissa started eating her turkey grilled sandwich. "Bishop Stevens thinks it's Maci Graham."

"She wasn't even here; that's ridiculous," Jody chimed in. "For obvious reasons, I think Bishop Stevens is more likely to be the suspect. His sister allegedly committed suicide because of Nathan, and Lydia was the ex who dumped him."

Ice looked between the two women, enjoying their take on the case.

"Interesting," Marissa shrugged. "But I think it's the wife, Terry Monroe. They should just lock her up already. That man has done her dirty for fifteen years. She finally snapped. Besides, Bishop Stevens is a good man. He is not capable of committing murder."

"Everyone is capable of committing murder," Ice said.

"True," Marissa conceded. "But not Bishop Stevens. He

is special."

"A pearl among men," Jody said sarcastically. "She has a crush on him. A huge crush spanning the four years she has been working with him."

"Keep your voice down," Marissa grimaced. "But you are right. I would make a good wife to that man. He is single, troubled and searching for love. I am the one he searches for."

Jody laughed. "Not if he is the murderer."

"I would visit him in jail," Marissa said, "wait patiently for him to get out."

"You can't be serious," Jody said.

"Hell no, I am not serious. I am not a 'pick me.' I like to fantasize, that's all. What is life without a fantasy or two?" Marissa chuckled. "Tell me about Saturday night. What did you see? What did you hear?"

"The police came to my door," Jody said, "they told me about the murders. I didn't hear any gunshots or anything like that from where I was."

"Boring," Marissa said. "I was hoping for more."

"I don't have more," Jody shrugged.

"There are some people in the admin pool that think you did it," Marissa said. "Just a heads up. Your name came up on their suspect's list."

"Me?" Jody squealed.

"Yep. There are rumors that you and Bishop Nathan had a thing."

"Good gosh," Jody put down her fork.

"The theory is Lady Monroe caught the two of you kissing in her office and fired you on the spot. And then, enraged by the unfairness of it all, you went after Nathan and killed him. Lydia saw you, and you killed her too."

Jody grimaced. "I don't know if I should laugh or cry.

Where would I get a gun?"

"You're from the ghetto," Marissa pointed out. "Everyone knows that's the breeding ground for gunmen. They have guns stashed everywhere down there."

"Ridiculous," Jody said dismissively. "If I wanted to kill anyone, why would I kill Nathan? Mrs. Monroe is the one I would be mad at for firing me."

"That's what I told them," Marissa nodded. "Why would you kill your supposed lover? Doesn't make sense."

"One of the girls said she heard Bishop Nathan calling you his one true love!"

"Fake news," Jody said exasperatedly. "I hate being the subject of gossip."

Ice smiled at her reassuringly. "I believe you, Jody."

"Me too," Marissa said loyally.

"I am going to take this to go," Jody said. "I am too upset to eat anything else, and my twenty minutes is up."

She left the table.

"What I am worried about," Marissa said to Ice as she watched Jody leave, "is that they can make her a scapegoat. I think whoever did this is high up on the food chain. It wouldn't be hard to get something like this to stick on a secretary."

Ice nodded contemplatively. "You may be right."

"They'll do it," Marissa said. "They'll just run with the 'she's from the ghetto' angle, or she hired one of her bad man friends to do the deed. Listen, if someone wants her taking the blame for this, the sheep will help them along, mark my words."

"Not under my watch," Ice thought. They'd be messing with the wrong secretary.

Chapter Twelve

Ice went into the office early on a Tuesday. He wanted to take a thorough look around Nathan's office before anybody came to question him snooping around.

Nathan's temporary secretary, Phedora, had popped in periodically yesterday. She had caught him sifting through Nathan's desk and had asked him aggressively, "What do you want?"

She was a battle-ax of a woman with a stern demeanor and a ferocious frown.

She did menace well. He might have been intimidated if he were really Pastor John Shepherd, grief counselor. Instead, he had looked at her exasperatedly because he knew how to improvise in a situation like that.

"Why can't I find anything in this place? I am just trying to find some sticky notes. Didn't Bishop Nathan have a sticky notepad? This office is frightfully neat."

"Untidy offices are frowned upon here," Phedora had

said fiercely. "Miss Graham said you would only be in this office temporarily. Someone will come by shortly to give you stationery and then when you leave the office will be cleaned for the next occupant."

He didn't think he liked Phedora much. She was not impressed by him one iota.

She made a growling sound whenever she saw him.

He looked at the bookshelf, taking the books one by one and flipping through them. There were lots of Tawny Monroe's books in there and lots of tomes that were religion-based. Their pages looked brand new. He could bet that Nathan Monroe did not read much, and these books were just for show.

He looked behind the paintings. Most were abstract, with greens and purples being the dominant colors. He wondered if Nathan chose those colors or if the paintings came with the office.

He hit the jackpot under the third painting. There was a safe, an electronic one. It needed a password to get in. Did all the offices have safes, or was this one unique? And what was the code to unlock this safe?

He wanted to see what was inside before anyone else could do so.

Thankfully, Wiley Securities was the company responsible for securing the Monroe Ministry building. They would know about the safe.

He called Chanelle quickly.

"I'll call you right back," she said excitedly. "He could put all sorts of things in a safe that he doesn't want to keep at home, especially in a building that is so protected."

Chanelle called two minutes later.

"Yep, all the offices on the second and seventh floors have safes. The codes are created by the occupants of the office.

Their maintenance department has the override keys. We don't keep them."

"Now that sucks," Ice whistled.

"You'll have three attempts at guessing the password, then it will shut you out. The passcode is usually six numbers," Chanelle explained.

"Three tries," Ice mused. "Mmm, what did this guy love most in the world?"

"Lydia," Chanelle chuckled.

"When is her birthday?" Ice stepped toward the picture, took it down, and rubbed his hands together.

"The third of the sixth, nineteen ninety-one."

Ice punched it in, and he heard a thwack sound as the light at the top turned green.

"I can't believe it," he murmured. "That's it!"

"What's in there?" Chanelle asked.

"A stack of papers, a diary, and a voice recorder. Let me take a picture and call you back," Ice said.

He took out the stack of notes. They were handwritten notes sent to him by Lydia. There were about twenty of them. She put hearts instead of dots on her "i's." Most of them were love notes, saying things like, "I miss you so much" and "I feel like a thirsty woman in a desert."

He carefully laid them out on the desk and photographed each one. Then he put them back in the stack and combed through the diary. It mostly contained appointments, errands, and plans for a vacation.

He quickly combed through it, finding two plane tickets at the back with his and Lydia's names. They were planning a trip to Hawaii.

He put the journal and notes back. He would sift through them later.

Next, he picked up the recorder and pressed play.

"I am trapped," Nathan's voice sounded slightly garbled. The sound of a breeze was in the background as if he were outside. "I cannot live an authentic life. I don't know what to do."

Ice searched through the audio files. There were fifteen of them on the recorder. He clicked on the one entitled "My plans."

"So here is what I am going to do," Nathan said into the microphone. His voice was clear and strong. "I am tired of living a double life, pretending to be happy. I am going to leave it all behind. This is no way to live. If I only had a year with Lydia where we could live without fear and hiding, I would be happy. Terry won't miss me; she does her own thing. The boys might blame me and say I messed up their lives. Am I selfish? Isn't it better to have a father who is not moping around in silent despair? Who finds it difficult to live like this? I don't want to live the rest of my life without Lydia by my side."

"My mother is going to kill me for this, but I find that with each passing day, I don't care anymore. Bring it on, whatever the future holds."

"Wow," Ice whispered. He copied the voice files and then put everything back in the safe.

He combed through Lydia's notes to Nathan. He found three of them to be interesting.

Hey love, this is it. I have stopped playing around. No more games. No more trying to replace you with anyone else. I tried. You are irreplaceable. I broke it off with Zahir; you should stop flirting with his sister to make me jealous. The girl is unstable. Love Always, Lydia.

Hey love, I like writing you notes. At least this way I can

be assured that no one is spying on us, and when I say no one, I mean Maci. She is relentless. I think Mom put her up to it. I doubt it's a coincidence that after kicking me out of their guest house, Mom offers the townhouse as an alternative and then moves Maci beside me. They are working together.

Maci is Mom's emissary. I think she is coming into my place when I am not there and searching through my things. I am going to prove it. I am going to keep leaving my spare key under the mat. She knows that's where I keep it, she watches my every move like a hawk.

Mark says he knows a guy who has high-quality hidden cameras with sound and video. I told him it was for my car, but it was really for my house. I am going to catch Maci Graham red-handed."

Hey love, I got Mario James from maintenance to install the cameras. It's funny how Maci took a picture of him leaving my apartment in the early hours and is again spreading falsehoods that I am sleeping with him. I want to clear it up with Mom, but I can't. I don't want her to know about the cameras. So we'll let the latest rumors about me slide. I am on the verge of catching Maci red-handed. I cannot wait.

PS. We need to discuss where to store the recordings. It has to be top secret because some of them will be freaky when you come over.

Nathan, I don't know how to tell you this, so I am writing it. I had a one-night stand with a friend. It wasn't supposed to mean anything; we got carried away. Please don't be mad. You were talking about ditching me for your peace of mind. He had issues, and I have issues; it just happened. Now I am pregnant. I don't know if it's yours or his. I will not treat this as bad news. I want kids. I have always wanted them. Please don't be mad.

Ice didn't know how he dialed Chanelle's number so fast. "I hit the jackpot!"

"What is it?" Chanelle asked urgently.

"Lydia had hidden cameras all over her apartment and in her bedroom."

"Sweet sugar pine loaf," Chanelle muttered. "That's awesome. There may be actual footage of who did this."

"That's right," Ice said. "Did the police find any cameras?"

"No," Chanelle said. "No cameras were logged into evidence."

"That means they are still there," Ice said. "I need to find where the data is stored, I have to find where Mario put the cameras."

"If you solve this in a week, it will be a record for us," Chanelle said. "Saint may just give you half his kingdom."

"Not interested; I love my job." Ice looked at the notes. "I am sending the notes to you shortly. In one of them, it seems as if Lydia is pregnant."

"She has a history of miscarriages dating back to her late teens," Chanelle said. "Who is the father this time?"

"She said it's a friend or Nathan." Ice whistled. "But it's Lydia we are talking about, so who knows who the candidates are?"

"I wonder if that's related to why she was killed?" Chanelle asked. "That's an angle we didn't think about."

"Right," Ice sighed. "This case is full of angles. Anyway, we are on the verge of cracking it. I need to get the video evidence."

"Keep up the great work," Chanelle said gleefully. "We are on our way to a record here."

"Oh, I just thought of something I would want," Ice said.

"What's that?" Chanelle asked.

"A simple request, really. I want you to hire Jody Fyre. I know you sit in on the interviews with Max, and he defers to you where this is concerned."

"Jody Fyre," Chanelle said. "You were really attached to that girl, weren't you?"

"Yes, I was, and I am. If she works for Wiley Securities and in your department, I will not need to hide who I am ever again. I want to have a normal relationship with her."

"I see," Chanelle said.

"She was fired on Friday because she saw and heard things she shouldn't have. I need to find out what Tawny Monroe is preventing her from saying, but for now, she needs another job. Tawny asked her to stay back for a month to help her finish a book, with a promise that she will give her a glowing recommendation for her next job."

"We don't need a glowing recommendation from Tawny Monroe," Chanelle said. "Give me her number. I'll call her personally to get the ball rolling."

****

Ice found Pastor Mark McGowan in the cafeteria, eating a hearty breakfast. The breakfast options were just as bountiful as the lunch menu.

He was just as confused as at lunch, and he didn't have Marissa to help him choose, so he did what he would have done at home. He got a green juice blend and a stuffed breakfast sandwich—it had everything he loved.

He went to join Mark, uninvited. Mark looked up at him and smiled. "How are you this morning, Pastor Shepherd?"

"Curious," Ice said. "What type of video recorder did you

recommend for Lydia to put in her... er, car?"

"The latest model," Mark said without blinking an eye. "It has superior technology and advanced features. It offers high-definition recording, excellent image stabilization, and user-friendly controls. We got it to check on our pets when we were not home. Trust me when I tell you it captures clear and detailed footage, even in low light."

"Good," Ice nodded. "Thanks."

"How did you know about it?" Mark asked. "Lydia said she had top secret reasons for getting it and couldn't tell anyone why, including me."

"I found out, by the way," Ice said. Then he lowered his voice, "Just how good a friend were you to Lydia?"

"We were working on a music project; we've been friends since I started working here five years ago. She wanted to explore her musical talents; as I told you before, she could have been an awesome singer or producer. She had talent." Mark looked around, "What are you implying?"

"I am not implying a thing," Ice shrugged. "They put me in Nathan's office, and I found a note Lydia wrote to him; it mentioned you."

"Me?" Mark looked afraid; there was raw fear in his eyes.

So, he was the friend Lydia had a one-night stand with, he had figured as much.

"Yep," Ice nodded.

"It was just a night, one silly night, three months ago," Mark whispered fiercely. "My wife just had a baby; Lydia just had a flare-up with someone she was seeing. We got carried away. Oh, God." Mark looked down at his plate refusing to look up.

"Why is it so difficult to be faithful?" Ice asked, "Self-control is not that difficult."

Mark covered his face. "What did the note say?"

"She told Nathan that you might be the baby's father. Did you know about the pregnancy?"

Mark groaned. "No, not at first, but I told my wife about the one night we spent together, and she said she overheard Lydia talking about cravings. She's the one that figured it out. It has been hell at home since then. She is literally losing her mind over this."

"Did you kill her?" Ice asked.

"No," Mark looked at him fiercely, "I am not a killer."

"You were in the army, and those shots were accurate," Ice said, "quite marksman-like."

Mark opened his mouth and then closed it. "I didn't kill her; that's not who I am. I have three kids under four years old. I can't afford to go to jail and leave them for their mother to raise alone.

"I'd really like to know who did it, though, because despite our single lapse in judgment, Lydia was a good friend, and I really want justice for her, and Nathan of course."

"Of course," Ice nodded.

****

"**I** told Linton about the hidden cameras," Chanelle told Ice when he was on the way back to the office. "He said he will join you at the apartment at eleven tomorrow. Most people should be at work, so your cover won't be blown."

"Cool," Ice said. "I just spoke to Mark McGowan."

"The friend from the note?" Chanelle asked.

"That's right." Ice said. "He is now at the top of my suspect's list. It seems as if it was indeed a one-night stand. He cheated on his wife, and Lydia got pregnant; that's a big motive if you ask me. He lives in the townhouse section. It's an easy slip in and out of Lydia's place."

"I'll check to see if he has a firearm."

"Good. I am visiting both Tawny Monroe and Terry Monroe at home today. I have no idea how long that will take. I heard that Tawny Monroe had a breakdown in front of cameras. I want to find out how genuine that was, and I need to see Terry. It's always good to see the spouse of the deceased, feel her temperature on things, find out how happy or sad she may feel about her dearly departed."

Cassius was in the seventh-floor lobby, on his phone, when Ice exited the elevator. He hung up when he saw Ice.

"You're back!" Ice said.

"I can't stay home," Cassius said. "Tawny is nagging me about doing something about catching the killer. And so, I told her about you."

Ice grimaced. "I was going to visit her today. She is on my suspect list."

Cassius glared at him. "That's preposterous."

"Is it really, though?" Ice asked. "She has the most to lose if word got out that her children are sleeping together. She writes books about family cohesiveness and togetherness and being a model family. And yet, her son, a married bishop, a senior member of your organization, was planning to run off with his only sister."

"We'll talk about this in my office," Cassius said tiredly.

Ice didn't say a word more until they were in the office.

Cassius sat in his chair. "Go on."

"Where were you Sunday morning at two am?" Ice asked.

"In bed, sleeping," Cassius said.

"Where was Tawny?"

"I don't know," Cassius shrugged. "We sleep in separate rooms. We have always done that. It's not that we have problems. That's just our tradition. Sometimes we sleep together, sometimes we don't."

"I see," Ice nodded. "So you don't know where she would be then?"

"I can't swear for her," Cassius said, "but what I can say is that Tawny loves her family. She may not always show it, but she does love us fiercely. She would not kill her own son; I can tell you that. Her solution to keeping Nathan and Lydia apart would not be killing them. Commit them to an asylum, yes. Lock them away in a room somewhere, kill them, no."

"Does she own a firearm?" Ice asked.

"She does," Cassius nodded, "and so do I."

"Do you know where Nathan's laptop is or Lydia's?" Ice asked. "I am assuming they both had computers?"

"Yes, they did. I haven't the faintest clue where those are," Cassius said. "Maybe it's in their cars."

"Both cars are parked in front of the townhouse?" Ice asked.

"Yes," Cassius nodded. "Do you need a search warrant for that?"

"No," Ice said, "it's in the process of an investigation. The head detective for the case will be meeting me tomorrow. We are looking over the townhouse one more time. Can you get me those spare keys? I'll have our IT department pick them up. I want to see what's on the laptops."

"I will arrange it," Cassius nodded. "Who else is on that suspect list of yours, apart from Tawny?"

"Zahir Stevens, Mario James, Maci Graham," Ice said.

"Maci?" Cassius widened his eyes. "That doesn't make sense."

"She didn't like Lydia," Ice said. "They had a competition going on for your affections."

Cassius sighed. "That has gone on for years. I am a father figure to Maci. Lydia liked being my only daughter and has always been jealous of Maci. Lydia is the one who had hang-ups about Maci, not the other way around. Why would Maci kill both her and Nathan?"

"I don't know yet," Ice shrugged.

"Mario James does some stuff for us at the house," Cassius said contemplatively. "He was Tawny's favorite graduate from our Rehab and Renew the program."

"Funnily enough, the ex-con was not my first suspect," Ice mused. "Too obvious."

Cassius nodded. "I see."

"I notice you didn't have anything to say about Zahir," Ice stood up and walked to the window.

"I don't know," Cassius murmured. "I firmly believe that anyone is capable of anything. He was engaged to Lydia, but then she broke it off with him. He is an ambitious young man; I could see him running this place in a couple of years. Maybe when Lydia ended it with him, and Nathan was unfairly linked to his sister committing suicide, he snapped. It's logical to assume he would kill them, but I don't see him doing that."

"And then again, I don't know anything anymore. That's why I hired you."

"I appreciate your input, nevertheless," Ice said, heading to the door. "I have to run; I have a hectic day ahead."

Chapter Thirteen

Jody had her earphone jammed firmly in her ear and was listening to her favorite playlist. It was nice not to have Mrs. Monroe in the office. She could hum to Chronixx's song "I Can." It was her daily anthem. It had been King's favorite song, and it became hers. She always felt a rush of warmth when she heard it; she thought about King.

She could sing a few lines without having to check herself. "When I look at where I'm coming from, I know I'm blessed, and I close my eyes and smile…."

She turned up the song and sang along; she loved the beat. She needed to find the book specifications for Mrs. Monroe's cover designer. He had called for it. She usually kept that in her book file. She got up to search for it and did a little jig as she searched through the filing cabinet.

"Sometimes I'm lost and far from home, but I'll find my way," she continued singing, "follow my heart and know I'll be found someday…."

She always imagined that King would say that when she sang it as if they were his own words.

"I Can by Chronixx," she heard behind her.

Jody spun around, her heart beating a mile a minute. She hadn't seen him since lunch yesterday. She had missed him.

"Pastor Shepherd," she pulled out the earphone from her ears.

"I love that song," he said. "Something about it is so positive and uplifting."

Jody smiled. "I don't know of any pastor in this building who would admit that out loud. Everybody pretends that any other music, but gospel is beneath them."

"Their loss. They are missing out on a host of good music." He smiled at her, and she felt a flutter near her heart.

"I'll be out of the office for most of the day," he said. "Is it too soon to say this? I'll miss you."

"I'll miss you too," Jody found herself admitting.

"Maybe we can walk later. I've been meaning to check out the recreational facilities."

"Yes, sure," Jody nodded.

"It's a date," he smiled. "Seven o'clock."

She nodded. "I'll be ready."

"By the way, my friend Chanelle Lewis will be contacting you about a job."

"Oh, really?" Jody looked at him excitedly.

"And we can go and check out that townhouse I told you about this weekend," he said.

"I... I don't know what to say," Jody whispered.

"Thank you would be sufficient; nothing else expected," he grinned. "You are blessed."

He left the office, and she closed her eyes briefly, trying to steady her racing thoughts. It was too soon, much too soon, to know this, but she felt as if Pastor John Shepherd would be significant in her life.

She felt a little pang of regret when she thought about King. She had loved him even though they had only been friends, and a part of her would always wonder about him—where he was now and what would become of him. And maybe that would never stop. But she had to be honest and frank with herself. She was twenty-four years old. Pastor Shepherd was an attractive man, and she was interested in him.

Maybe it was time she put her youthful fantasies of King to rest and embrace the man who was now in her life. They clearly liked each other. It was time to move on.

****

The Monroes lived in the same neighborhood where Ice had his house. It was also where his aunt and his cousins, Charles and Blaine, had their property. At one time, his uncle Edgar Payne had owned most of the hill, and his parents had secured a few pieces for themselves and their children. His parents and sisters had sold theirs. He hadn't been inclined to do so. After law school, he always knew he would return to Jamaica.

The neighborhood was far from what it used to look like back in the day. It had been more rural. Today, it was a hotspot for the rich and famous. The Monroe house was modest compared to the grand structures around them. It was on a half-acre of land, with a lovely front and back garden.

He pulled up at the gate and pressed the buzzer. He was promptly let in when he said he was Pastor John Shepherd.

"Mrs. Monroe is expecting you," her housekeeper, a stout Indian woman, said. "She is by the pool. Follow me."

Tawny was lounging by the pool in a voluminous dress that seemed to swallow her slim frame. Oversized square shades framed her eyes.

"Hello, Mrs. Monroe," he said.

"Sit," she pointed to a chair across from her.

He sat. "How are you doing?"

She removed her glasses; her eyes were red and swollen. "Do you know what it's like to lose a child, Pastor Shepherd?"

"No," Ice said, "I can't say I do."

"Well, it hurts," Tawny sniffed. "I hurt. All over. I cannot breathe without the pain choking me. I think about the two of them, night and day. I remember when Nathan was a baby and a toddler, how bright he was. I remember Lydia when she was trying to pronounce the word 'confused,' and she always ended up saying 'confood.' I am devastated."

Ice cleared his throat. "I am sorry for your loss."

Tawny looked at him teary-eyed. "Who would want to harm my babies?"

"They weren't babies, Mrs. Monroe. They were grown folks who had a physical relationship with each other while they had other relationships. Nathan was married and had children. He was unhappy with the status quo. They were planning to go away together. Anyone could have wanted them gone."

Tawny's tears miraculously dried up, and she grunted. "You are right. They were not babies anymore. They wanted to destroy this family and all that we stood for. I would have lost them through death or otherwise. Nathan was hell-bent on pleasing his selfish desires instead of looking at the bigger picture.

"It doesn't stop me from remembering when they were innocent and unproblematic," she said softly. "I would have preferred if they had run away. At least I would have known that they were still alive. There are many ways you can spin them not being around anymore. Parents are not supposed to bury their children. It's unnatural."

Ice sighed. "It's tough, I can imagine."

"Did Nathan know that Lydia was not his biological sister?" Ice asked.

Tawny sighed. "My husband told you that?"

Ice nodded. "I need to know as many facts as possible to see this case through. The more I know, the better."

"My carefully crafted secrets are just tumbling out of the closet for all to see," Tawny inhaled. "Nathan knew, but he only found out a few days ago. He was threatening to leave his wife and his children. He said he would kill himself if he couldn't be with Lydia."

"And I told him, 'Nathan, Lydia is not even your biological sister. Why would you kill yourself over that?'

"He lost it. He went berserk. He yelled at me, accused me of deceiving him for years, and called me other choice names. It wasn't pretty. It was downright awful, the things that came out of his mouth. My secretary heard all of it."

"And you fired her the next day?" Ice asked.

"I did," Tawny sighed. "Jody is a lovely girl, but I cannot be around her after she heard what Nathan said. I don't expect her to tell anyone because of the nondisclosure, but it was awful, and I cannot..." her voice trailed away. "I was a terrible mother."

Ice sat back and watched while she quietly sobbed.

"Did Terry know about Nathan and Lydia?" Ice asked when Tawny wiped her eyes and was silent for a while.

"I doubt it," Tawny said. "She did know he was with someone. I don't know who she thought it was. How did my family become such a mess?" She asked. "Ordinary non-religious families don't have this kind of drama. Why is the devil attacking us like this?"

She wasn't directing her question to him, so he didn't respond.

"All I wanted to do was help these children who didn't have a mother or father. We should have been one happy family. Instead, our lives are little more than a soap opera. It begs the question, doesn't it? Was it all worth it, all of this? I never had a close relationship with any of them, really. Benjamin hated me as a baby. He instinctively knew I wasn't his mother. I was ecstatic when I had my own son. I thought this would be my chance to have a child that loves me."

Tawny blinked back tears. "And Nathan preferred his nanny to me. When Nathan was a baby, do you know how many nannies I hired and fired? Until I just gave up. The twins and Lydia weren't much better either. It's as if I have some sort of child repellent."

"It's a pity they don't come with manuals, do they?"

Ice watched her as she talked. She didn't need his input.

"Maybe it would have been better if I didn't have children. There wouldn't be the pain of losing them now, would there?"

"Mrs. Monroe," Ice said gently.

"Call me Tawny," she sniffed.

"Tawny," Ice continued. "I would recommend a real grief counselor. Someone who can guide you through this."

"I don't want anyone to know how messed up my family life is," Tawny sniffed. "I can't let anybody in."

"You will have to," Ice said gently. "The need to be perfect can be overwhelming and isolating. Opening up to a grief counselor can provide a safe space to express your emotions and work through your challenges. Understandably, you don't want anyone to know about your family's struggles, but keeping everything bottled up inside can be detrimental to your well-being.

By seeking help and sharing your true story, you might find a sense of relief and support from others who have experienced similar situations. It's important to remember that being 'normal' doesn't mean hiding your true self or pretending to be someone you're not.

"And when you write your next book, 'Tawny Monroe's Guide to Living an Imperfect Life Perfectly,' I'd read it."

Tawny looked at him contemplatively. "Thank you."

"Don't mention it," he smiled at her. "Where were you in the early hours of Sunday morning?"

"In my bed sleeping," Tawny said. "I take my melatonin by 10 pm and I am out like a light by eleven. Constance, my housekeeper, can back me up on this. We have a routine. We always pray together, meditate, and then I take my nightly melatonin drink. I find it difficult to fall asleep otherwise. You can ask her on your way out."

He did ask Constance on his way out.

"Yes, she was here on Saturday night," Constance said. "Miss Tawny has a very predictable routine. We usually pray together. We started doing that years ago when I started working here."

"That's nice of your employer to pray with you," Ice said.

"If it wasn't for Miss Tawny, I wouldn't be here," Constance said. "I was beaten and left for dead, and I still have no memory of it. Miss Tawny was visiting the hospital where I was, and she took a liking to me. When I got better, she invited me to work here."

"So you don't remember anything about your previous life?" Ice asked incredulously.

"Nothing," Constance said. "Zero. We've been praying for God to restore my memory, among other things. In our prayer sessions, Miss Tawny always prays for her children and grandchildren. She mentions them one by one. She would never harm them."

"I hear you," Ice nodded. "Well, have a good day."

"You too, Pastor Shepherd," Constance smiled.

Chapter Fourteen

He didn't know how to feel about Tawny Monroe as a suspect after he visited her. She obviously had an obsessive-compulsive need to keep up appearances. But would that be a good enough reason to kill her children? She seemed genuinely distressed at the thought of their deaths, but was that grief remorse? Was she mourning or sorrowful that she killed or had them killed?

His instincts told him it was her, but having met and interacted with her, he was left confused.

It was a mere three-minute drive from Cassius and Tawny's house to Nathan and Terry's. He had called ahead to speak to Terry.

"The boys are in school," she said when she greeted him at the door. "I gave them the option of staying home or going to school. They chose school. Nolan is on the football team, and they have a match today. And Nesbeth has chess club. Their school provides counseling services. They are fine."

"And how are you?" Ice asked. Terry looked painfully thin, almost frail, like a good gust of wind could blow her over. It didn't help matters that she was in all-black: leggings and a tightly fitted blouse that outlined her rib cage in sharp detail.

"I am good," Terry said. "I am not grieving. I told my father-in-law this when he insisted I see you. He said I should be open and honest with you about everything. That's something I never thought I would hear from the bishop. They are not big on being open and honest in this family."

"May I ask why you are not grieving?" Ice looked around the living room. It was decorated in warm earth tones, and family pictures were everywhere. If he didn't know the background of this family, he would imagine they were very close by the sheer volume of photos on the walls.

"Have a seat," Terry said, pointing to one of the comfortable sofas.

She sat before him. "I'm not actively grieving Nathan as a husband or partner. I grieve because he is the boys' father. They won't have him in these crucial years. I probably will cry at the funeral when it hits me that he's gone forever and will no longer be here for them. The truth is, our marriage has been over for years now.

"To pretend as if I'm heartbroken would just be hypocritical. The police already quizzed me about where I was and what I was doing on the night of the murders. It's to be expected, I guess. I am the spouse. My husband cheated on me constantly. I was probably thought to be driven by jealousy when I caught him with his sister.

"I was nowhere near Lydia's apartment. I was practicing with the choir. We were having a music extravaganza the following Sunday, and I had a lead role in one of the songs."

Ice cleared his throat. "You knew about Nathan and

Lydia?"

"Yes, I did," Terry nodded. "I first suspected them years ago. I didn't want to believe it. I was in denial. It was his sister, I said. I thought he was just being a possessive big brother, and unusually close to his little sister. When she got married, he went a little crazy and I thought that was not normal. My brother would not act like that about me, like some sort of jilted lover.

"Anyway, all my fears about the two of them were confirmed when Lydia and Charles, her ex-husband, divorced. I asked Charles if the reason for the divorce was that he caught them, and he said yes. He didn't elaborate. And, contrarily, I felt relieved. I had a reason for why my husband felt distant and why he was so unloving, and why his sister was the one who got all of his attention. I weighed the pros and cons of staying with Nathan, and the pros won."

"But why stay?" Ice asked, confused.

"The boys," Terry shrugged. "His parents asked me to hang in there. A second divorce on the heels of Lydia's divorce was not a good look for the ministry, besides the added stigma of being a divorcee. Yes, that is still a thing in this day and age, especially when you're connected to a prominent church family."

Ice frowned. "I had no idea that's a thing."

"It is," Terry nodded. "Besides, I like Monroe Ministries. I like working there. That's where all my friends are. It is a community I appreciate, and I don't want to upset the status quo. I was Bishop Nathan Monroe's wife and was treated accordingly. The point is, I was quite fine with our life the way it was. He lived his way, and I lived mine. I am not unhappy. Maybe if I found someone else, I would have pushed for change, but I haven't."

Ice nodded. "Did he tell you he was planning to run away

with Lydia?"

"No," Terry widened her eyes. "He wouldn't!"

"He would," Ice nodded. "He was planning to divorce you, and they would run away together and live where no one knew they were brother and sister."

"That stupid, stupid man," Terry growled. "We discussed divorce two years ago. He said he would not even consider it before the boys were grown. I can't believe this. If anything, I would have thought he would be busy with his latest fling, not Lydia."

"His latest fling?" Ice asked.

"Whoever is Tawny's secretary," Terry said. "I don't remember her name. It is Fire, I think, but spelled with a 'y.' I don't really keep up with his women."

"They were never an item," Ice said through gritted teeth. "I think that rumor needs to die."

"I don't really care about that," Terry shrugged. "I can't believe he was planning to leave me after we had an agreement. Well, now I feel betrayed. I would have been the jilted wife instead of a widow. Seems as if someone did me a favor."

Ice sighed. "I wish you didn't say things like that, Terry."

"I wish my dead husband wasn't worse than excrement. We can't all get our wishes, now can we, Pastor Shepherd?"

Chapter Fifteen

Ice knocked on Jody's door. It was seven minutes after seven. He had reached home, showered, and put on a tracksuit. He was feeling a bit keyed up. He had returned to the office and played the part of grief counselor. Nobody he had talked to after lunch was a suspect. Most of them spouted the same tired platitudes, "Bishop Nathan was such a nice man; Miss Lydia was the best."

He needed to cleanse his palette with a Jody visit and to take advantage of the opportunity to see her as much as possible after going nearly six months without her. She looked through the peephole and then opened the door.

"Hello, Pastor Shepherd," she said.

"Call me John," he smiled.

She was dressed in a t-shirt and tight black leggings that molded her slim curves. It was the second time he was seeing her dressed so casually. Yesterday was the first. All their encounters had been after work when he had been undercover in Black Lane. He had forced himself to leave her alone on the weekends. And that had been a struggle. He had not wanted anyone to pinpoint her as his special friend.

"Would you like to go for a walk? Or a drive?" he asked. "Dinner? Movie?"

Jody looked down at her bare feet and laughed. "I just ate leftovers from yesterday. And the rest of my ice cream. A walk it should be."

Ice nodded. "Then a walk it is."

Monroe Ministries had a one-mile walking trail on the outskirts of their recreation area. There was also a field where people played football and well-lit tennis courts, which were all occupied.

"I am going to miss this when I leave here," Jody said wistfully. "I have been meaning to learn to play tennis."

"I can teach you," Ice said. "We can get in as many sessions as possible before you leave here. There is a tennis court at the townhouse where my friend is offering for you to stay."

"Thank you," Jody smiled. "I have three weeks and four days to go. Do you think I can learn it that fast?"

"Sure," Ice said confidently. "With dedication and regular practice, you can definitely make significant progress in three weeks. Besides, I'll find you wherever you are, and we can put in a game or two and hone those skills."

"Not if I go to Westmoreland," Jody said. "I have been thinking of finding a job and living with my family there."

"That will not be necessary," Ice said. "I know of a job. My friend Channelle said she would personally contact you shortly. They are actively looking for someone at the moment."

Jody stopped walking and looked at him. "On the one hand, I think you are too good to be true; on the other, I am wondering if it's all a lie. It's so hard to trust people these days."

Ice grinned. "I am a pastor; why distrust me?"

"No offense, John," Jody said, frowning, "but I am not as trusting of your profession as I used to be. As a matter of fact, I think that you guys have too many issues."

Ice chuckled. "Which profession do you think is perfect then, Jody? Every profession has its flaws and challenges."

"I know, but I need some distance between what I heard last Thursday night to even look at your profession favorably again."

"You mean the mysterious conversation you overheard with Tawny and Nathan that you cannot speak about?"

"It wasn't a conversation; it was a shouting match," Jody wrinkled her nose, "laced with profanity and crude language. And the things said... I can understand why Mrs. Monroe doesn't want me around anymore. Her family is rotten to the core."

"I spoke to Tawny today," Ice said. "She alluded to that too."

Jody looked around him. Nobody was close to them, only a woman about a quarter mile ahead and a couple walking fast half a mile ahead.

"Can I trust you with this, John?"

Ice looked at her and nodded. "You can trust me."

"I don't know why I feel like I can," Jody sighed. "You remind me so much of King. I miss him so much... I could tell him this."

"You can tell me," Ice said. "I can be your King replacement."

"No one can replace King," Jody said fiercely.

"Now I am affronted," Ice said, smiling. "This King guy seems larger than life. I cannot compete."

"Sorry," Jody said. "I gave myself a speech about letting

him go and moving on. It's been six months; why can't I?"

Ice felt like hugging her to him and never letting go. Bless her loyal, loving heart. What they had before meant something to her too.

"Then don't let him go," Ice said. "What you had with him was special. He obviously meant a lot to you. That kind of feeling is rare in this world."

Jody stopped walking. "He was a criminal. How can I love a criminal, put my life on hold for him? I am so confused."

He wanted to tell her he was King, but he couldn't. He had to change the subject.

"Hello, peeps," a cheerful voice said behind them.

They both spun around. A pretty lady with long braids and a cheerful smile greeted them.

"Hey, Francesca," Jody greeted her warmly.

"Jody Fyre and…"

"Pastor John Shepherd, grief counselor," Jody introduced.

"Oh yes," Francesca stepped on the spot. "My husband told me about you. I am on maternity leave, and I've been giving the building a break."

"Yes, he told me about you too," Ice smiled, "he called you his warrior princess."

Francesca smiled. "These days it's more like princess mom. I just had our third girl."

"Congratulations," Ice said.

Francesca smiled. "Family is everything."

Ice nodded. "So you can appreciate how Bishop Monroe and his wife feel."

"Oh yes, my heart goes out to them," Francesca said. "You guys are walking too slow for me. I have ten thousand steps to get in and some baby weight to get off."

She gave them a jaunty little salute and walked off.

"What did she do over at Monroe Ministries?" Ice asked.

"She is in charge of the day care center, and she is the children's choir leader. They won an award the other day. She's everybody's friend. We can't talk here if I am to tell you anything about Thursday night, not with her zooming around the field. She walks scarily fast. No wonder she looks like she lost the baby weight already."

Ice nodded. "Okay then, we'll drive somewhere away from here."

****

"**K**ing taught me to drive," Jody said when she got in his car. "I learned to drive on the busiest streets in downtown Kingston and at night, too," she chuckled. "I would practice parking in the empty parking lots of the businesses down there. I got my license six months ago; I wish he was around to see it."

Ice glanced at her. "Congrats on getting your license. Where is King now?"

"I don't know," Jody sighed. "If I could just tell him goodbye, I'd be okay. I would feel better and move on. I wouldn't keep looking over my shoulder, expecting that he is watching. I can't believe he would abandon me like this. I always thought that what we had was solid, you know?"

"I know," Ice tightened his fingers on the steering wheel. "You need closure."

"That's the word," Jody nodded. "Anyway, enough about me. We should be talking about Thursday."

"Thursday," Ice nodded.

"It was late last Thursday night. I stayed behind to work with Mrs. Monroe on her speech for the Magnolia Girls Home. They were celebrating a milestone anniversary. Parts of it would be televised; Mrs. Monroe likes seeing herself on the news."

Ice chuckled.

"Anyway, she finally signed off on the final draft. I was supposed to type it up and email it to her the next morning. She likes to memorize her speeches so that she doesn't appear to be reading from notes. She's really good at doing that too. I sometimes marvel at her ability to do that. I think she has a partial photographic memory or something."

"Anyway, I was leaving for the night, and when I reached the apartment building, I realized that I didn't have the speech. I had to go back for it. When Mrs. Monroe says she wants something first thing in the morning, she means first thing."

"So I went back. Downstairs was busy; there were all sorts of choir rehearsals, dress rehearsals for Sunday's music extravaganza. I even saw some famous people. I saw C. Wiley!"

Ice grinned. "I know Case Wiley."

"Really?" Jody squealed. "I can't believe it."

"He's a good friend," Ice said. "A cool guy, but you were talking about Thursday night."

"Oh yes," Jody said. "Anyway, I went upstairs, and as soon as I stepped out of the elevator, I heard yelling."

"Nathan Monroe was calling his mother some choice words at the top of his voice. When I came on the scene, he screamed, 'You are why I am like this, Mom. This is all your fault!'"

"Nathan, calm down," Mrs. Monroe said, "lower your voice."

"I will not be calm," Nathan growled. "My whole life, you tell me what to do, where to go, who to see, who to marry, which career to have, how to raise my children. I have no autonomy; I am a puppet. You run this whole family like it's an extension of you. Well, I am tired of it. I am forty-five years old. If I cannot run my own life at this stage, I might as well kill myself. You have ruined me."

"I didn't hear what Mrs. Monroe said to that," Jody said. "I figured it was along the lines of 'How have I ruined you?' Because he started enumerating everything. I can't remember some of it; it was a lot. I remember him talking about not loving Terry when they forced him to marry her, but Terry is a bishop's daughter, so they thought it would be a perfect match.

"He spoke about Lydia, his sister, being the first woman, he ever loved."

"Wow," Ice said. "Shocking!"

Jody glanced at him. "You don't sound shocked."

"I am not," Ice murmured. "I heard that was a possibility recently."

"I was shocked," Jody shook her head. "I still am. But what got me shook was when he said Lydia was pregnant."

Ice slowed to a crawl. "Oh really?"

"But," Jody paused dramatically, "maybe it wasn't his child. He wasn't sure because Lydia had a one-night stand with Pastor Mark McGowan."

Ice pulled over at the side of the road. "Mark McGowan, obviously."

"Yes," Jody nodded. "He said Lydia had too many miscarriages before, so she would keep this child whether it was theirs or not. They would raise it together."

"And then Mrs. Monroe said, 'I can't allow you to continue with this immorality, Nathan.' Her voice sounded tired. 'You are an adult; you can choose to live a better life. You have a perfectly good wife and two wonderful sons, and you are talking about Lydia, your own sister as if you two are star-crossed lovers.'"

"'I love her, and I don't care if she is my sister!'"

"'She is not your sister!' Mrs. Monroe shouted. "And I rue the day we adopted her. She has brought nothing but shame and disgrace upon us. I despise that girl, she is nothing but pure evil, and I despise you because you cannot see it.'"

"What do you mean she is not my sister?" Nathan asked. "What are you saying, mother?"

"I made a noise, made my presence known," Jody said, "and went for the notes. Mrs. Monroe looked devastated. I hurriedly exited the office, but not before Nathan went off on a tirade. He called his mother some unrepeatable names, and she called him some too. She even said, 'You are dead to me, Nathan.' I don't know who I hate more, you or Lydia. You both sicken me.'"

"And she fired you the next day," Ice murmured.

"Yes, and I think she did it," Jody whispered. "I think she couldn't live with the fact that Nathan wanted to run away with Lydia, who was pregnant with another married Bishop's child. She was a woman at the end of her tether."

"Interesting," Ice murmured.

"She begged me not to tell the police. And I think I know why. She doesn't want to be a suspect. Am I destined to be protecting criminals? Is that my life's work?"

"No, you are not," Ice said sympathetically. "The thing is, we can't be sure if she did it. People say things when they are angry all the time. As for King, you don't know if he is a criminal. Sometimes things are not what they seem."

"And sometimes they are," Jody snorted. "I tend to see the best in people and make excuses for them. I am a criminal magnet."

Ice chuckled and started the car. "You are not a criminal magnet. How many criminal friends did you attract while living in that neighborhood of yours?"

"Just one," Jody shrugged. "A big one. Maybe I am a large criminal magnet. Where are we going?"

"Lookout Point, to see the city lights and talk about everything else but Monroe Ministries, King, and the murder mystery in our midst. We'll get to know each other. I want to override the King file you have saved on your hard drive."

He winked at her.

Chapter Sixteen

Cassius Monroe sent the spare keys to Lydia and Nathan's car in the morning. It was a little after seven. Ice was already dressed and ready for work. Ironically, Cassius sent over the keys with Mario James. Maybe Cassius wanted him to question the man further?

"The bishop said you needed these," Mario handed him the keys.

"I do," Ice took them.

"Why do you need the two of them?" Mario asked. "You can't drive two cars at once."

"I need to check both cars for something," Ice said. "I need it to do my job."

"Oh," Mario nodded. "Well, okay then."

He moved away.

"Wait," Ice said, closing his door. "I've been meaning to talk to you."

Mario nodded. "I know."

"Do you have time now?" Ice asked Mario.

"I do," Mario nodded. "I have to fix the fountain at the front; one of the pipes is blocked."

"How are you feeling today?" Ice asked. "You looked quite out of it on Monday."

"I was really shocked on Monday," Mario said. "It's just now beginning to sink in that Lydia is gone. The truth is, I didn't know Bishop Nathan that well, but Lydia was always nice to me."

"Were you having an affair with her?" Ice asked as they walked toward the townhouses and the cars.

"No," Mario said. "No affair. She was involved with someone, and I have a girlfriend."

"Do you know who Lydia was involved with?" Ice asked.

"Not a clue," Mario shrugged. "I hear things, but I have this policy to believe none of what I hear and only half of what I see."

Ice chuckled. "I've always liked that saying."

"I literally had to do it," Mario said. "Drugs addled my brain, scrambled my senses; I literally can't trust them. I would be dead now if it weren't for the Monroes, especially Miss Tawny. She saved me from returning to the streets when my family kicked me out."

"What did you do before the drugs and jail?" Ice asked him as if he didn't already know. Channelle had sent over a profile on him.

"I was an electrician," Mario said.

They walked towards Lydia's townhouse. Her car and Nathan's were still parked side by side. The crime scene 'do not cross' tape was still around the small lawn at the front.

"Such a waste of life," Mario said. "I will always remember Miss Lydia as forever pleasant and optimistic about life."

Ice nodded. When he reached the cars, he opened them

with the key fob. He searched Nathan's car first and found his laptop in the back seat on the floor under a briefcase. Lydia's laptop was in the passenger seat under her mat.

Mario watched Ice curiously as he took the two laptops and locked the cars.

Ice dearly wished one of them had the data feed for the cameras.

"You installed the system for Lydia, didn't you?" Ice asked Mario.

"Yes," Mario nodded.

"Could you show me where?" Ice asked.

Mario frowned. "I can just tell you; I don't want to go in there. Thinking about what happened makes me squeamish. The cameras are in every bulb socket, even in the bathroom. Miss Lydia insisted on it."

"Thank you," Ice nodded.

Mario nodded and stepped away.

He called Chanelle as soon as Mario left. "I have the laptops."

"I'll send Troy for them," Chanelle said. "Fingers crossed; we can figure out the passwords as easily as you did with the safe."

****

Jody woke up with a sense of well-being, a smile on her face, and a happy jaunt to her steps. She had spent most of the evening with John. It was the most fun she had had in months. They had a lot in common. He was easy to talk to and could possibly replace King in her affections. And best of all, she had finally shared her worst fear, that Tawny Monroe was the one who killed her children.

It felt like a load had been lifted off her shoulders. She

would use today to adjust her resume and peruse some online job listings. Ice said she should expect a call from his friend Channelle but until that came through, she would be looking.

She had never gotten a job by applying for one. This was going to be a new experience. Her job with Yanique Thelman had been a referral by her school principal, Vanessa Whitman. She had worked in the principal's office as a student worker. Vanessa was friends with Yanique and recommended her when she graduated.

Yanique had recommended her to Tawny Monroe.

However, she didn't see Tawny Monroe recommending her to anyone. How would she explain why she didn't want her around anymore? Jody was a good worker but knew too much about her dysfunctional family and her children's nasty, immoral lives.

Jody inhaled tremulously. Despite the fact that she would have to job hunt on her own for the first time, it was a beautiful Wednesday morning, just slightly overcast and breezy.

She knocked on John's door and got no response. Maybe he had already left for work. She knew she would see him sometime later in the day, so no worries there.

It was a little earlier than she normally would be going to work, especially since Mrs. Monroe probably wouldn't be in the office. Maybe she would have an extended breakfast. She knew she would find Marissa in the cafeteria. They could have a morning chit-chat.

She would miss her morning and lunchtime chit-chats with Marissa, but there were Marissas in every workplace. At Thelman and Associates, her work friend had been Gayle. At Monroe Ministries, it was Marissa. Who knows who it will be next?

Marissa was indeed in the cafeteria when she got there.

She had a heaping plate of pancakes with all the toppings as usual.

Jody went for toast, eggs, fruit, and requisite celery-kale juice.

"And you wonder why you feel sleepy by ten o'clock," Jody said, glancing at Marissa as she covered the stack of pancakes with maple syrup.

"Hey," Marissa grinned. "I was thinking about you just now."

Jody smiled. "What were you thinking about me?"

"I was thinking how much I will miss you when you are gone."

Jody nodded. "I was thinking the same. We can still keep in touch."

Yep," Marissa nodded, "but it won't be the same."

"I know," Jody said.

"You will be leaving luscious Pastor Shepherd to the likes of me."

"He and I can still work," Jody said. "I am going to be looking for jobs in Kingston; it's not like I am going to be in a different parish."

"Drat," Marissa grunted.

Jody laughed. "He is a very nice person."

"He is, and handsome too," Marissa said. "Some of the girls from admin went to him for grief counseling, even though they are not grieving."

Jody chuckled. "I imagine that would happen."

"He didn't encourage any of them," Marissa said.

"Good," Jody nodded.

"On the bright side, they no longer think you are a suspect," Marissa said. "Unfortunately, my poor Bishop Stevens is now ruling the suspects' list in their little gossip club."

Jody giggled. "I am not surprised."

"Along with Terry Monroe, somebody saw her smiling yesterday, and they concluded that it was a smile of satisfaction. That poor woman will never smile again without somebody thinking she did it."

Jody shook her head. "Never."

Marissa rambled on and on. They finally finished breakfast and went their separate ways.

Jody was about to press a button on the elevator panel when her phone rang.

"Jody Fyre, this is Chanelle Lewis from Wiley Securities," Chanelle said. "Pastor John Shepherd gave me your number; he said you are seeking a job."

"Yes!" Jody said eagerly. "I am."

"Please send me your resume. I texted you my address. Would this Friday be okay for an interview?"

"Yes!" Jody said. "Oh, yes!"

"Great," Chanelle said briskly. "I will email you back with a time."

Jody couldn't quite believe it. She literally sailed to the office; she was so excited.

Her excitement, however, was brought down a notch when she walked in and saw Tawny Monroe sitting at her desk.

"Mrs. Monroe, how are you?" Jody greeted her. She really wanted to ask, what are you doing here? And did you kill your children?

"I've been better," Tawny said wearily. "I realize I am not the sit-at-home-and-grieve type of person. I have to be busy."

"I decided something, Jody."

"What is it?" Jody entered the office and sat in the chair across from her desk.

"I'm going to scrap the current book I am doing." Tawny said. "You and I both know it's rubbish. My family is not a good shining example of anything. As a matter of fact, we are quite possibly more dysfunctional than the average family. I am going to write a new book. I don't know what I will entitle it yet, but it should be along the lines of Monroe Family Secrets and How it Got My Children Killed."

"Wow," Jody whistled.

"Or, We are Not Perfect, Tawny Monroe Confesses All."

"Will you be confessing all?"

"Everything," Tawny said. "From how I met Cassius, the true story, to how Lydia was adopted to the fact that Maci is Simon's child. I am tired of the rumors about my husband and Mariam."

Jody gasped. "What?"

"When I am done," Tawny said, "nothing will be left in our closet. You can leave by the end of the week if you want, or you can stay. What you know or don't know doesn't matter to me anymore. I'll be telling everyone anyway."

"Er," Jody swallowed, "I was just about to send my resume to a company. I have an interview on Friday."

"Whatever you decide is fine by me," Tawny said. "You will get a glowing recommendation from me, nevertheless. Thank you for holding down the fort these last two days. My first task for you this morning is to find me a reputable therapist."

"What about Pastor Shepherd?" Jody asked.

"He's good. I saw him yesterday. He is why I am here now, prepared to bear it all," Tawny said. "But I need much more than what he has to offer at the moment."

Chapter Seventeen

Ice walked through Lydia's townhouse with Detective Linton, his partner Detective Grey, and two other plainclothes officers. The cameras were in every light socket, as Mario had said. They were still active and inconspicuously placed. No one would know they were there.

"So, you think the computers have the feed?" Linton asked Ice.

"Yes," Ice nodded.

"Well, after you guys crack the code, let us know," Linton said.

"Of course," Ice said, "I think video evidence will bring closure to this case."

"As usual, love working with you guys over at Wiley Securities," Linton pumped his hand vigorously.

Ice frowned, "I have no clue what you are talking about, sir. I am Pastor John Shepherd."

Linton laughed, "I doubt you'll be Pastor Shepherd for

longer, but I stand corrected. I shouldn't be blowing your cover."

Ice exited the townhouse and almost bumped into Maci. She was standing in her driveway curiously looking next door. She was dressed casually, if a tad warmly, in a hoodie and socks.

"Pastor Shepherd, what's going on over there?" Her voice sounded stuffy.

"Nothing much," Ice shrugged. "I thought you would be at work at this hour."

"I think I have the flu," Maci sneezed into her kerchief.

Ice stepped out of her way. "You should go in and lie down," he told her gently. "Drink up your fluids and try not to stress."

"I was lying down when I heard voices and then saw the police car," Maci sneezed again.

"Where does Mark McGowan live?" Ice asked, walking toward Maci's house.

She followed him. "Mark McGowan lives in townhouse twelve, around the corner."

"How often did he visit Lydia?" Ice asked.

"I have never seen him visit," Maci sniffed. "His wife Francesca visits, though. Sometimes she carries the kids. Lydia loves kids. I think she was a godmother to one or the two of them, I don't know."

Ice nodded. "That's one positive thing you have said about Lydia. Congrats."

Maci rolled her eyes and then groaned. "My eyes hurt."

Ice opened her door. "Go and get some rest."

"Wait a minute," Maci asked, "how is the case going?"

"I found out that you liked to snoop in Lydia's house when she is not there."

"Lies!" Maci said weakly. "I wouldn't do that. That

sounds like something paranoid Lydia would accuse me of. Practically, everybody knows that she keeps her spare keys under her front mat, if someone was snooping it wasn't me."

Ice smiled. "Go get some rest, Maci."

****

"**H**ow was your day?" He greeted Jody at her door a little after seven. "I haven't seen you all day."

"My day was surprisingly good," Jody said. "Mrs. Monroe is back."

"I heard," Ice nodded.

"And she said I could stay on if I wanted to, but your friend called today from Wiley Securities, and I sent over my resume. And now I am torn; I don't want to leave just when you got here."

"Let's walk and talk about it," Ice said. "And look at the pros and cons."

Jody nodded happily.

They set off walking. "One big pro of working with Wiley Securities is the pay package. It's heftier than here, but I have free housing and free breakfast and lunch here, and I do not have to take a taxi to work," Jody said. "However, Wiley Securities is quite close to a university. I can do evening classes and finish my degree in business administration. I have just two years to go."

"My friend's apartment is not far from Wiley Securities," Ice said. "That's another pro. There is subsidized lunch at Yum Yum Café, another pro, and you can always carpool with other employees in the vicinity until you get your own car. Admittedly, I see no cons working away from here."

"I am getting excited just thinking about it. The job description sounds fun," Jody said. "I will be going for an interview on Friday at eleven."

"Good for you," Ice said. "I know you will ace the interview; I can take you. We can have lunch afterward."

"Such a pity, though, you just got here, and I like you," Jody said.

"I like you too, but you leaving here won't be a problem. We'll manage to see each other whenever we want to. I drive, you know," Ice grinned. "Who knows, I might also work at Wiley Securities one day."

"They need grief counselors there?" Jody raised an eyebrow.

"In this world, there is a need for grief counselors everywhere," Ice grinned.

"You are a miracle worker, and quite good at your job," Jody said wonderingly. "Mrs. Monroe said you made her see sense, and she is turning over a new leaf. She had me searching for a therapist today. I didn't know her son-in-law was a therapist. She said he was the best but that she couldn't use him because he would probably run if he heard her coming."

"I doubt that," Ice said. "Charles is a professional. One of the best in the business. He is also a psychiatrist. So there's that."

"You know him?" Jody asked.

"Quite well," Ice nodded. "It's a small world."

"I don't think she is the killer anymore," Jody said, "if she is willing to expose it all…"

"You two lovebirds," Francesca said behind them, "strolling as usual."

Jody spun around. "Francesca!"

Francesca walked ahead of them and then started walking backward. "Yes, it's little old me, getting my steps in, trying to see if I can fit into my old outfits before returning to work in a couple of weeks."

"By the way, Pastor Shepherd, I saw you with the police today at Lydia's apartment. What on earth is going on?"

"The head detective wanted my feedback on something," Ice said. "I gave him my professional opinion. I do consult with the police from time to time in my capacity as a counselor."

"I see," Francesca nodded. "I think I am suffering from PTSD. When I saw the police cars again, I had a little panic attack. What happened was so disconcerting in our normally quiet community."

"Do you want my services?" Ice asked. "I can be of help, you know. I already saw your husband, and Maci told me you were a frequent visitor to Lydia's place. I know you must be missing her."

"She was more Mark's friend than mine," Francesca said. "She loved the kids. I am afraid they were the main attraction, not me." She glanced at her fit watch. "My heart rate is coming down; got to take it back up a notch."

"I did not know Francesca and Lydia were friends," Jody whispered when Francesca left. "I guess the saying is true, opposites attract."

"How were they opposites?" Ice asked.

"Well, Lydia more or less kept to herself, and Francesca is outgoing and friendly. Lydia was more secular, and Francesca more spiritual," Jody explained.

Ice nodded contemplatively.

"Well, at least that's the vibe I got from both women. Neither of them is my friend," Jody said and then looked at him. "Are you thinking what I am thinking?"

"That Francesca McGowan didn't seem like she was grieving?" Ice asked.

"No," Jody laughed. "I was thinking that we're moving too

slowly. We need to kick it up a notch."

He agreed with her. They were moving too slowly. He wanted to kick it up a notch. He had treated this woman as his friend for two years, he loved her without compare, and he was impatient for her to know who he was and for them to kick it up a notch for real.

"Tell you what," Ice said, picking up the pace. "I'll drop you off at your interview on Friday. We'll look over the apartment in the evening. I'll help you move on Saturday. We'll get married on Sunday and have a family by Monday."

Jody started laughing, panting a little. "Now you are going too fast. I can't keep up with the walk and the weekend itinerary."

Ice slowed down. "Sorry."

Jody laughed. "I'll take up the offer for Friday, though."

Ice nodded. "Right."

Chapter Eighteen

The interview with Chanelle and Max went great. Jody knew she had made a good impression, especially with Chanelle.

"We deal with a lot of sensitive information here," Chanelle said. "Sometimes our cases are literally life or death. When we send an operative to cover a case, we fully support them."

"We already did a background check on you," Chanelle leaned forward. "Your life is surprisingly clean. Is there anything else you would like to tell me?"

Jody inhaled. "I, well, I had a relationship of sorts with a gangster. We were just friends, but I..."

"Oh," Chanelle smiled. "Milo's lieutenant, King."

"How did you know?" Jody asked.

"We know things," Chanelle leaned back in her chair. "Are you in touch with this gangster?"

"No," Jody shook her head. "I am not."

"What would you do if he came back into your life?"

Chanelle asked.

"I don't know," Jody said honestly. "I know nothing of his work. He didn't tell me anything about that. I would like to see him one more time to tell him goodbye. He was quite a good friend to me. He... we... it would be goodbye. I could move on."

"Are you sure it would be just goodbye?" Chanelle asked. "You sound really attached to this guy."

"It would be goodbye," Jody said firmly. "I am interested in someone else."

Chanelle chuckled. "Well, is the person you are interested in Pastor John Shepherd?"

"Yes," Jody nodded. "He told you?"

"Yes," Chanelle nodded. "He is a good guy, one of the best."

Chanelle cleared her throat. "I'll let you know what we decide by this evening. If you were hired, would you have a problem starting on Monday?"

"No problem at all," Jody said.

"Well, good. It's nice to meet you, Jody," Chanelle shook her hand.

Jody exited the building feeling optimistic about the whole interview. John was waiting for her by the car at the front of the building.

"How did it go?" He asked.

"Great!" Jody gushed. "Chanelle reminds me of Yanique, my previous employer. I think she is badass to work in a male-dominated field like this."

Ice smiled. "I'll tell her you said that."

"So where are we off to?" Jody asked.

"We can go and see your new townhouse and then find something to eat, and then we go back to work."

"Sounds fun," Jody grinned.

****

The townhouse was indeed ten minutes from the Wiley Building. It had three bedrooms and a little garden at the back. It was tastefully furnished and had everything, even dish towels and unopened soaps, in the bathrooms. It was clean as a whistle, not even a speck of dust anywhere.

"I can't believe it," Jody said. "Are you sure that your friend wants me to live here rent-free?"

"Yep," Ice nodded. "I am also negotiating with him for you to use his car."

"Are you serious?" Jody sat down on the settee and looked around. "Who is your friend, and how can I thank him personally? I mean, this is a lot to do for someone he doesn't know."

"His name is Irving Carlisle Ellis Junior," Ice sat across from her. "I don't think I want you to meet him just yet. He'll fall instantly in love with you, and you'll forget about me."

Jody laughed. "That won't happen. Trust me, I am not that frivolous. I am not even over King, and that was six months ago."

Ice smiled. "I keep forgetting about your great love affair with King."

"It wasn't a love affair, well, not the way you understand love affairs. We didn't have a physical relationship," Jody sighed. "I told Chanelle about him."

"You did?" Ice frowned. "Why?"

"It's an intelligence agency; they deal with security. I had contact with him. He is not exactly an upstanding member of society."

Ice winced. "And what did you say to Chanelle about him?"

"She asked me what I would do if he came back into my life. I told her I would say goodbye."

Ice nodded. "And close that chapter."

"And close that chapter," Jody said wistfully.

"It's sad when people leave without saying goodbye, isn't it?" Ice murmured. "It leaves a lingering sense of unfinished business, a void that's hard to fill. I felt that once. I had to leave someone without saying goodbye too. I didn't like it one bit."

Jody looked at him curiously. "You never talk about your previous relationships."

"I had a few," Ice shrugged. "Only one significant one. She is the person I couldn't forget because I didn't say goodbye to her either."

"So we are basically in the same boat," Jody said.

Ice chuckled. "Yes. Maybe that's why we found each other. Let's go eat; I am starving."

****

Chanelle did not let her wait too long before calling her after the interview. "Jody, you are hired. We sent you an official email. Monday is your start date; come prepared to hit the ground running."

Jody returned to the office after lunchtime and told Tawny Monroe immediately. Tawny was resigned to the news. "It's our loss, their gain."

She packed her personal things from the office that evening and was moved into her new apartment by Saturday. She still couldn't believe how fast everything was going and how blessed she was.

John spent most of the day with her. They ordered food, and they hung out. They ended up watching a movie until late evening and falling asleep in front of the television.

"I should go," Ice stood up and yawned. "The apartment won't feel the same without you next door."

"Don't be friendly with the person who will move in beside you," Jody said jealously.

Ice smiled and kissed her on the cheek. "I won't."

Jody felt the kiss long after he left.

Chapter Nineteen

"**I**rving Carlisle Ellis," Chanelle said loudly in his ear on Sunday morning. It was barely light out. "You have to get in here."

"To the office?" Ice asked, confused.

"Oh yes," Chanelle said. "We cracked the password for Lydia's video feed. She was really good with the password. She used upper and lower cases and mixed them up with numbers. It took our experts quite a while but decode it they did."

"Have you seen who did it?" Ice asked excitedly.

"Yes," Chanelle said. "I think our case is closed."

"Who is it?" Ice asked.

"I am not going to tell you over the phone," Chanelle snorted. "Get in here."

Ice made it back to the office in record time. Saint and Max were there. They looked just as sleepy as he felt.

"All I have to say is, Lydia Monroe was hardly home,"

Chanelle said, "and when she was, ooh child, drama. I will not bore any of you with our various footage. Lydia did indeed have someone who was snooping around. It was this lady here."

"Francesca," Ice whistled. "Francesca McGowan, Mark McGowan's wife."

"That's right," Chanelle said. "She was looking for something specific."

"Maybe evidence that her husband was having an affair with Lydia?" Ice murmured. "Lydia and Mark had a one-night stand. Lydia was possibly pregnant with Mark's child, as well as it could be Nathan." Ice explained for Saint and Max's benefit.

"And then there is this," Chanelle pointed to a clip where Francesca was trying on Lydia's clothes and sobbing in her closet. "She wrote the name slut across the mirror and then rubbed it out. Her phone rang, and she answered it.

"How could you cheat on me with her, Mark? What does she have that you don't have at home? I am leaving you and taking the kids! I hate her, and I hate you for letting this happen. I don't care if it was just one night. Doesn't commitment mean anything to you? "

She left the house in Lydia's dress and had to turn back to remove it and put on her own.

And then the final video clip, last Sunday morning.

"Why do you always do this to me?" Lydia turned tear-streaked eyes to Nathan. "I thought we were moving towards being faithful to each other. We promised that there would be no one else! And I caught you with yet another one of Mom's secretaries."

"You didn't catch me doing anything," Nathan said tiredly. "I had a mental break on Thursday. Mom fired her on Friday because she heard most of it, and so I went to apologize. Set her straight on some of what she heard. You can go and ask her if you don't believe me."

Lydia sat across from Nathan in the living room. "Look at us; we are no good together."

"But we suffer when we are apart," Nathan said wearily. "I suffer when you are not around; I suffer when you sleep around."

"The pot calling the kettle black." Lydia laughed. "You are just as bad as me."

"Actually, I am not," Nathan said seriously. "I pretend to sleep around to make you jealous. You actually do it. You are a slut."

"But you love me," Lydia laughed, "and you'll do anything for me, your own sister."

"You are not my sister," Nathan stood up, "sorry to disappoint you. I know you like your sick little fantasies."

"What are you talking about?" Lydia sobered up long enough to ask.

"Mom told me you were adopted from a distant cousin of Dad's."

Lydia laughed. "I knew that. Her name is Emma, and she lives in the Cayman Islands. She had me when she was seventeen. She contacted me when I was eighteen to let me know."

"So why on earth haven't you said anything?" Nathan shouted. "I have been going around thinking how utterly worthless I am. Not only was I cheating on Terry, but I couldn't stay away from you. Things would have been different if I had known you weren't my sister."

"I liked the thought of you thinking that I was your sister. You felt extra dirty, and I liked it."

"You are sick!" Nathan growled. "All this time, we could have done something about us. I could have divorced

Terry and married you. We could live down the talk when everybody realized we are not related."

"Maybe I wasn't ready," Lydia shrugged, "but now I am. I have never had a pregnancy passing the three-month stage. I want this baby."

"The baby might not even be mine," Nathan said. "Why would I uproot my life for a woman who doesn't know the meaning of faithful to raise a kid that may be Mark McGowan's."

"No one will know he is the father," Lydia said. "I told him, and he was fine with it."

"You told him?" Nathan growled. "What on earth for?"

"Because until our little ill-advised one-night stand, he was my friend," Lydia said. "He deserved to know. Unfortunately, he confessed to Francesca about our night together and she has been coming into the apartment, trying on my clothes, and crying like a mad woman. I thought it had been Maci, but it's her."

"So that's why you hate Maci," Nathan said wonderingly. "She is a real Monroe, and you are not."

"Maybe," Lydia shrugged.

"I am going," Nathan stood up. "I don't know if I want to do this with you anymore. You are exhausting."

"You like exhausting. I am suddenly not attractive to you because you discovered I am not your sister. That's the real reason you are going."

"That's not true," Nathan growled. He grabbed her head and held her in a vice grip, "I love you. I don't care about anything else."

They started kissing passionately, tearing each other's clothes off frantically. They headed for the room, and we were lying in bed caressing each other when a shadowy figure dressed in black opened the front door and tiptoed into the room.

She shot Lydia first and then Nathan in the head.

"So sorry, Lydia," she whispered. "I can't have you running around with my husband's baby."

Then she removed the mask. It was Francesca McGowan.

Everyone collectively inhaled, even Chanelle, who had watched it already.

"I sent the video to Linton. He will be picking her up in a few hours. They need a search warrant for the premises," Chanelle said in the silence. "She was not on my list because she is not a gun owner, her husband is though."

"Her husband is the guy who gave Lydia the cameras?" Saint asked.

"He is." Ice murmured. "How ironic. He didn't realize it would be used against his wife. However, thanks to those cameras our case was solved faster than we expected."

"Congrats on getting this wrapped up in a week," Saint said.

"Good work, you two," Max patted him on the back. "I am going back to bed."

"Me too," Saint bumped his fist with Ice. "For a small infinitesimal minute, I expected the person to be Tawny Monroe."

"Me too." Ice said. "But I am happy it's not."

****

Jody couldn't escape the news on Monday morning. It was on all the stations. It had even made international news. Francesca McGowan was taken into police custody for the murder of Nathan and Lydia Monroe. The police have evidence linking her to the crime; the motive is not yet apparent.

The news was on all the banks of monitors in the Wiley Securities lobby area.

"That was fast," Jody said wonderingly when Channelle greeted her in the lobby. "I didn't even know the police were on it, I didn't see anyone around taking statements or anything like that."

"That's because we were on it," Channelle said jovially. "The bishop said he wanted to know who killed his children, and we delivered."

"Oh," Jody widened her eyes. "I didn't know you guys were working there."

"We were," Chanelle said, showing her to her new office.

Jody didn't even get to appreciate that she had her own working space—an honest-to-goodness office with her own desk, guest chairs, and file cabinets.

"Our operative who we sent undercover said you were quite helpful with the case; we appreciate that."

"You had someone undercover?" Jody frowned.

"Yes," Chanelle nodded. "Our best detective, Irving Carlisle Ellis, aka Ice, aka Pastor John Shepherd, aka King. I think you had more than a passing acquaintance with that particular persona."

Jody slumped down in her chair. "What?"

"You will be responsible for putting all the case files together for the Monroe case and collating all the evidence for the police. You'll be very familiar with the case then. By the way, welcome to Wiley Securities. There is never a dull day around these parts. Let me show you around and show you how we do things."

Jody's head was reeling, but Chanelle made sure that she didn't dwell on the shocking news. She had to focus. She didn't want to make a bad impression on her first day, but the fact that King was Pastor Shepherd and this Irving Carlisle

Ellis person who had her staying at his townhouse was mind-blowing.

He didn't come into the office that day, though she anticipated seeing him and telling him off.

When she exited the building that evening, she spotted him standing by an unfamiliar car.

He waved to her.

She walked over to him, a scowl on her face, and then the scowl melted into a smile. How could she stay mad at him?

He didn't have his glasses on. A tug of familiarity hit her as she looked into his eyes. They were King's eyes. Now that she had heard he was King, she could see it.

"Hello, Jody Fyre," he smiled.

"Hello, Irving Carlisle Ellis."

"Actually, I prefer Ice," he smiled. "Do you think I am a coward? I had Chanelle do the big reveal."

"No," Jody whispered, but there was no sound.

"Unfortunately, I could not tell you any of it before now," Ice said. "I have been waiting to wrap up this case before I could say anything."

"Jody?" he asked urgently.

She was just standing there, not moving.

"I missed you so much," Jody slid into his arms and hugged him tight. "I worried about you for months! I felt like I was cheating on you with Pastor John Shepherd, and then I forced myself to move on. You look so different!"

Ice's grip tightened around her, providing both physical and emotional support. "I missed you too, every day. I had no choice but to leave without an announcement. I never anticipated that I would think about you every single day for six months."

"I can scarcely believe this," Jody's voice trembled. She struggled to reconcile the image of the man she thought she knew with the intricate web of secrecy he had woven around himself.

Ice took a deep breath, his gaze locked with hers. "I could not break cover while in Black Lane. Milo's organization was deeply involved in illegal activities—drug trafficking, arms smuggling, and more. I was assigned to infiltrate their ranks, gather evidence, and bring them down from within. To tell you anything, to even hint at my mission, would have been to put you in danger."

Jody's mind raced, connecting the dots—his seeming difference to the men around him, the way he treated her respectfully.

"I never suspected any of this," Jody whispered, her voice filled with a mix of admiration and concern. "You risked everything to protect others."

Ice's eyes softened as he cupped Jody's face gently in his hands. "Jody, you mean everything to me. I had to find a way to get us on the same page after this case. I am so happy to finally share this part of my life with you."

Jody's eyes welled up with tears, a jumble of emotions swirling within her. She leaned into Ice's touch, feeling the warmth and love radiating from him.

"So, where were you today?" she asked.

"Cassius Monroe requested that I stick around. They found the murder weapon in Mark's office safe. Mark was shocked, he had no idea that Francesca did it.

"The ministry is in an uproar, understandably. And I had to pick up this car for you, Irving Carlisle Ellis Jr. wants you to have it."

"Aww, thank you, Ice," Jody looked at him and then the car and started crying. "I don't know if I will get used to this or call you Ice."

"You will," Ice said. "In a few years, we will be a regular

boring couple who knows everything about each other."

"Somehow, I doubt that," Jody smiled through her tears. "It will never be boring around you."

Ice reached out and gently wiped away Jody's tears with his thumb. He couldn't help but feel a rush of emotions as he looked into her teary eyes.

"You're right," Ice replied softly, his voice filled with warmth and affection. "Our journey has been anything but ordinary, and I wouldn't have it any other way. Now that I can be open and honest with you, I promise you this: I will always be by your side, ready to face whatever comes our way."

Jody's tears transformed into a mixture of joy and gratitude. She leaned in closer, resting her head against Ice's shoulder, finding solace in his embrace.

"Ice and Fyre," Jody whispered, "now and forever."

The End

Excerpt- No Surrender (Book Ten, Crimson Hill Series)

Gersham's suit itched. He wasn't used to formal clothing, and he had outgrown the last suit he had worn to a funeral. This monstrous, boxy thing was made from the scratchiest fabric imaginable. The stiff material seemed to conspire against his every move, provoking a constant battle between his skin and the constricting garment.

He tugged at the collar, desperately seeking some relief from the torment. Sweat trickled down his forehead as he questioned his decision to accept the suit from his well-meaning granduncle. He should have found the time to go shopping for something that didn't look like it had appeared on the cover of Gentleman's Quarterly 1876.

At least then, he wouldn't have stood out among the modern, elegantly dressed individuals at the funeral. Even now, with the smaller group in the library at the reading of the will, he was more conspicuous than ever.

Even Enid Rafferty's lawyer, who looked like he was pushing the edges of ninety, was dressed better than him and was probably feeling better too.

His discomfort only intensified as he noticed the scrutinizing gaze of Patti Sue. He knew she was laughing at him. He couldn't blame her; he would laugh at himself too. And to think this wretched suit he wore was all because he wanted to impress her. His granduncle had said he had an Armani suit for him that would make him look debonair at the funeral. Gersham had taken the outfit without looking at it.

He had been too busy leading up to the event. He had been the main caretaker for Enid Rafferty's yard and house, an unpaid volunteer role that had evolved over time because of his fondness for the old lady.

He spent most of his evenings caring for Enid's one-acre property when he finished work at the Silver Spoon restaurant he co-owned with his brother. He had considered it a labor of love and to keep Enid's company.

Since she died, her family, who didn't know much about how she operated, leaned on him for everything leading up to the funeral. Additionally, the Rafferty family had asked him to cater for the repast, and he had done most of the cooking for that, as well as picking up her various family members from the airport and supervising the cleaning of the house and getting it ready for guests.

He had not taken any time out to consider the suit. He had stared at the thing appalled when he had finally unwrapped it from the garment bag, but what could he do then.

He had to go to the funeral. He was one of the pallbearers. He had been closer to Enid Rafferty than anyone there; it would have looked odd if he didn't attend.

She had been like family to him. She was kind of like the grandmother figure he had never had. His relationship with her had even outlasted his relationship with Patti Sue, her niece. Enid used to have a good laugh at that.

Her fondest desire was for him and Patti Sue to get back together.

Come to think of it, that was his fondest desire too.

"Enid Rafferty considered all of you in this room to be near and dear to her." The lawyer cleared his throat.

Gersham looked around; there were seven of them in the library; it was Enid's favorite room in the house. Her brother, Gus, and his wife, Anne, her cousin, Marlene, and her husband, Fred, and Patti Sue.

It was a shrinking family. Enid's other brother Andy and his wife had died in a car crash when Patti Sue was a little girl. Enid had never married; her fiancé had died in a boating accident a month before the wedding.

"I will love him forever," she had told him simply, "no other man will ever measure up; why should I put myself through the misery."

It was kind of how he felt toward Patti Sue.

He glanced at her. Patti Sue had a heart-shaped face with soft, delicate features that seemed to embody innocence and vulnerability. Her eyes sparkled with warmth and kindness. Silky black curls cascaded down her shoulders, framing her face in a way that accentuated her beauty.

But it wasn't just her physical appearance that captivated him. Patti Sue possessed a genuine and compassionate soul that radiated from within. She loved to laugh. She found joy in every situation. When they were together, Patti Sue made him feel cherished, understood, and accepted for who he truly was. With her, he didn't have to pretend or put on a mask; he could be his authentic self.

He missed that. Good Lord, he missed it. He couldn't recreate it with anyone else.

Their breakup had literally sent him reeling. Everyone had said he would get over her. Even Patti Sue herself, but so far, four years and a couple months, he hadn't managed to.

He knew in his heart that he would love her forever; he would probably die single and lonely like Enid Rafferty. Even now, being in the same room with her brought its own set of itchiness somewhere in the region of his heart.

"Without further ado, let's go into the last will and testimony of Miss Enid Rafferty," the lawyer broke into his thoughts.

Gersham straightened up in his chair and fixed his collar, which felt as if it were choking him. He wondered what Enid had left for him, maybe her big wheelbarrow or temperamental grass cutter.

"To my brother Gus and his lovely wife Anne," the lawyer read, "I bequeath two million dollars to do with as you wish."

Everybody gasped.

He was sure it wasn't just him. There was stillness in the air, a puzzlement on each face. Where did Enid get that much money? His eyes met Patti Sue in mutual shock.

Gersham knew she obviously was not poor; she lived on the rich side of Crimson Hill with its big houses and big yards. And the house was well-maintained.

Just last year, she changed the roof and windows to a more modern style. It had never occurred to him that Enid had used her own money for it; he hadn't given it much thought.

"To my cousin Marlene and her husband Fred, I thank you for checking in on me through all these years and keeping the family link alive; I bequeath you two million dollars to do with as you wish."

Marlene and Fred were grinning from ear to ear.

Gersham almost choked when the lawyer looked straight at him and then at Patti Sue, "Now for the bulk of her estate."

Bulk? He almost swallowed his tongue. Estate?

"To Gersham, you are the son I never had. Thank you for the endless days of conversations, keeping me company without prompting, your selfless nature, and your willingness to help an old lady who was often alone and rambling about the past; you did it without compensation or force. You, sir, are a one-in-a-million type of man. And to Patti Sue, my sweet niece. I understood what being a mother would have been like when you came to live with me. I know at times we didn't see eye to eye, and I could be a little difficult to live with but know this, I love you and always will. I bequeath to both Gersham Silver and Patti Sue Rafferty my entire estate portfolio, which includes this house in Crimson Hills and my apartment complex in Kingston. I also want Gersham and Patti to share equally my stock portfolio, currently valued at ten million us dollars, and all the cash in my current savings and chequing accounts, at the time of this writing, valued at over sixty million dollars."

Gersham didn't move a muscle, he was probably in a dream, but his suit reminded him that this was no dream. He was still itching like crazy.

Discover Exclusive Offers and Be the First to Know!

If you haven't already, don't miss out on the opportunity to join my New Release Newsletter! Sign up today and become part of an exclusive community where you'll be among the first to hear about my latest book releases and take advantage of special prices.

Why join my mailing list?

Be the First: Get a head start and be the first to know when I release a new book.

Exclusive Discounts: Unlock special prices available only to subscribers. Enjoy limited time offers and save big on your favorite books.

Quick and Easy: Signing up takes less than 30 seconds.

To join, visit https://www.brenalbar.com/newsletter or scan the QR code below.

Thank you for your support, and happy reading!

Ridgeview Series

The Ridgeview series follows five couples on the Jamaican north coast in the luxurious community of Ridgeview. It explores their everyday struggles with careers, children, and family drama. Each book touches on love, marriage, and trust as the characters face challenges that test their relationships.

Ride or Die (Book 1)
Play For Keeps (Book 2)
Through Thick and Thin (Book 3)
Tried and True (Book 4)
Stay With You (Book 5)

Spice and Stone Series

Join three extraordinary girls—Cinnamon, Cayenne, and Sage—as they navigate the intricate flavors of life, love, and romance in the captivating Spice and Stone series.

Cinnamon (Book 1)
Cayenne (Book 2)
Sage (Book3)

The Crimson Hill Series

Where family drama, romance, and a touch of sci-fi blend seamlessly in the enchanting backdrop of a small town in Jamaica. Prepare to embark on an unforgettable journey as secrets unravel, passions ignite, and destinies intertwine.

The Wiley Brothers

Step into the world of the Wiley Brothers, where tragedy weaves an unbreakable bond and love becomes their guiding light. In this captivating series, follow the journey of six remarkable boys as they navigate the tumultuous path of growing up without parents, discovering love, and finding their place in a challenging world.

Between Brothers (Book 0)- How it all began…
For Pete's Sake (Book 1)- Preston's story.
Crossing Jordan (Book 2)-Jordan's story.
Fire and Walter (Book 3)- Walter's story.
The Perfect Guy (Book 4)-Guy's Story.
The Patience of a Saint (Book 5)- Saint's Story.
A Case of Love (Book 6)- Case's Story.

The Pryce Sisters

Follow the remarkable journey of the Pryce triplets as they navigate the complexities of growing up, discovering romance, and embracing the exhilarating challenges of the new adult years.

Baby For A Pryce- Book 1
Right Pryce Wrong Time – Book 2
Yours, For A Pryce- Book 3

The Jacksons

Prepare to be enthralled by the captivating saga of the Jackson family. In this gripping series, secrets unravel, paternity questions loom, and love blooms in the most unexpected corners.

Ace- Book 1
Deuce- Book 2
Trey- Book 3
Quade- Book 4

The Scarlett Series

Their patriarch died and unexpectedly left each of them a fortune. Watch as the Scarlett family navigate their way through the ups and downs of sudden wealth, family secrets, and the complicated dynamics of their relationships.

Scarlett Baby (Book 1)
Scarlett Sinner (Book 2)
Scarlett Secret (Book 3)
Scarlett Love (Book 4)
Scarlett Promise (Book 5)
Scarlett Bride (Book 6)
Scarlett Heart (Book 7)

Magnolia Sisters

They were the rejects. The worst of the lot, they grew up in a girl's home together and formed sisterly bonds. Each book in the series tells the story of a different girl and the unique struggles and triumphs she faces along the way. With themes of friendship, forgiveness, and the power of love, the "Magnolia Sisters" series is a heartwarming and inspiring read that you won't want to put down.

Dear Mystery Guy- Book 1
Bad Girl Blues- Book 2
Her Mistaken Dream- Book 3
Just Like Yesterday – Book 4

New Song Series

A group of friends started out as a church band, see how each of them navigate their personal and professional lives while staying true to their faith and facing challenges along the way. With themes of forgiveness, redemption, and second chances, the New Song Series is a captivating read for anyone who enjoys heartwarming stories of love and faith.

Going Solo- Book 1
Duet on Fire- Book 2
Tangled Chords- Book 3
Broken Harmony- Book 4
A Past Refrain- Book 5
Perfect Melody- Book 6

The Bancrofts

The Bancroft family delves into the inner workings of academia and the high-stakes world of university politics. The family wrestles with the pressures of maintaining their family's legacy, they must confront their own demons and navigate the complex relationships that bind them together. From unexpected love affairs and betrayals to scandals and secrets that threaten to tear them apart, this is a series that will keep you captivated until the very end.

Homely Girl- Book 0
Saving Face- Book 1
Tattered Tiara- Book 2
Private Dancer- Book 3
Goodbye Lonely- Book 4
Practice Run- Book 5
Sense of Rumor- Book 6
A Younger Man- Book 7
Just To See Her- Book 8

Three Rivers Series

Three Rivers Series, a captivating tale of love, redemption, and second chances set in a picturesque community in St. Ann's Bay, Jamaica.

Private Sins- Book 1
Loving Mr. Wright- Book 2
Unholy Matrimony- Book 3
If It Ain't Broke- Book 4

The Resetter Series

The Resetter Series takes a look at a rare kind of person, a person who can travel back in time, but they only have one chance to get things right if they go back! With themes of second chances, changing the past and the power of love, the resetters series is a captivating time travel romance that many readers have described as a page turner.

Never Too Late- Book 1
Never Say Never- Book 2
Now or Never- Book 3
Almost Never- Book 4

On the Rebound Series

Experience the gripping and emotionally charged On the Rebound series, where love, betrayal, and redemption collide in a whirlwind of passion and secrets. Brace yourself for a journey filled with drama, cheating scandals, DNA questions, and ultimately, the power of second chances and finding love again.

On the Rebound- Book 1
On the Rebound Book 2

Standalone Books

Full Circle- After graduating from university, Diana wanted to return to Jamaica to find her siblings. What she didn't foresee was that she would meet Robert Cassidy and that both their pasts would be intertwined, and that disturbing questions would pop up about their parentage just when they were getting close.

After the End- Torn between two lovers. Colleen married her high school sweetheart, Isaiah, hoping that they would live happily ever after, but life intruded, and Isaiah disappeared at sea. She found work with the rich and handsome Enrique Lopez as a housekeeper and realized that she couldn't keep him at arm's length.

Love Triangle: Three Sides to the Story- George, the husband. Marie, the wife, and Karen-the mistress. They all get to tell their side of the story.

New Beginnings- Inner-city girl Geneva was offered an opportunity of a lifetime when she learned that her 'real' father was a wealthy man. Her decision to live up-town meant she had to leave Froggie, her 'ghetto don,' behind. She also found herself battling with her stepmother and battling her emotions for Justin, a suave up-towner.

The Preacher and the Prostitute- Prostitution and the clergy don't mix. Tell that to ex-prostitute Maribel, who finds herself in love with the Pastor at her church. Can an ex-prostitute and a pastor have a future together?

Historical Fiction

You won't want to miss out on these two captivating reads!

"The Pull of Freedom" tells the story of a slave family and their desperate struggle for freedom in Jamaica's colonial era. Follow the journey of these brave individuals as they fight for their right to be free, facing danger, heartbreak, and unimaginable obstacles along the way.

"The Empty Hammock" takes readers on a journey through time, as a modern woman finds herself transported back to the Taino era of Jamaica's history. Experience the wonder and mystery of this ancient culture through her eyes, as she learns about their traditions, beliefs, and way of life. With richly drawn characters and a beautifully realized setting, "The Empty Hammock" is a must-read for anyone who loves historical fiction that transports them to another time and place.

Short Story Collections

Di Taxi Ride and Other Stories- Funny stories about Jamaican life to make you laugh.

www.ingramcontent.com/pod-product-compliance
Lightning Source LLC
Chambersburg PA
CBHW051831150726
47998CB00001B/376